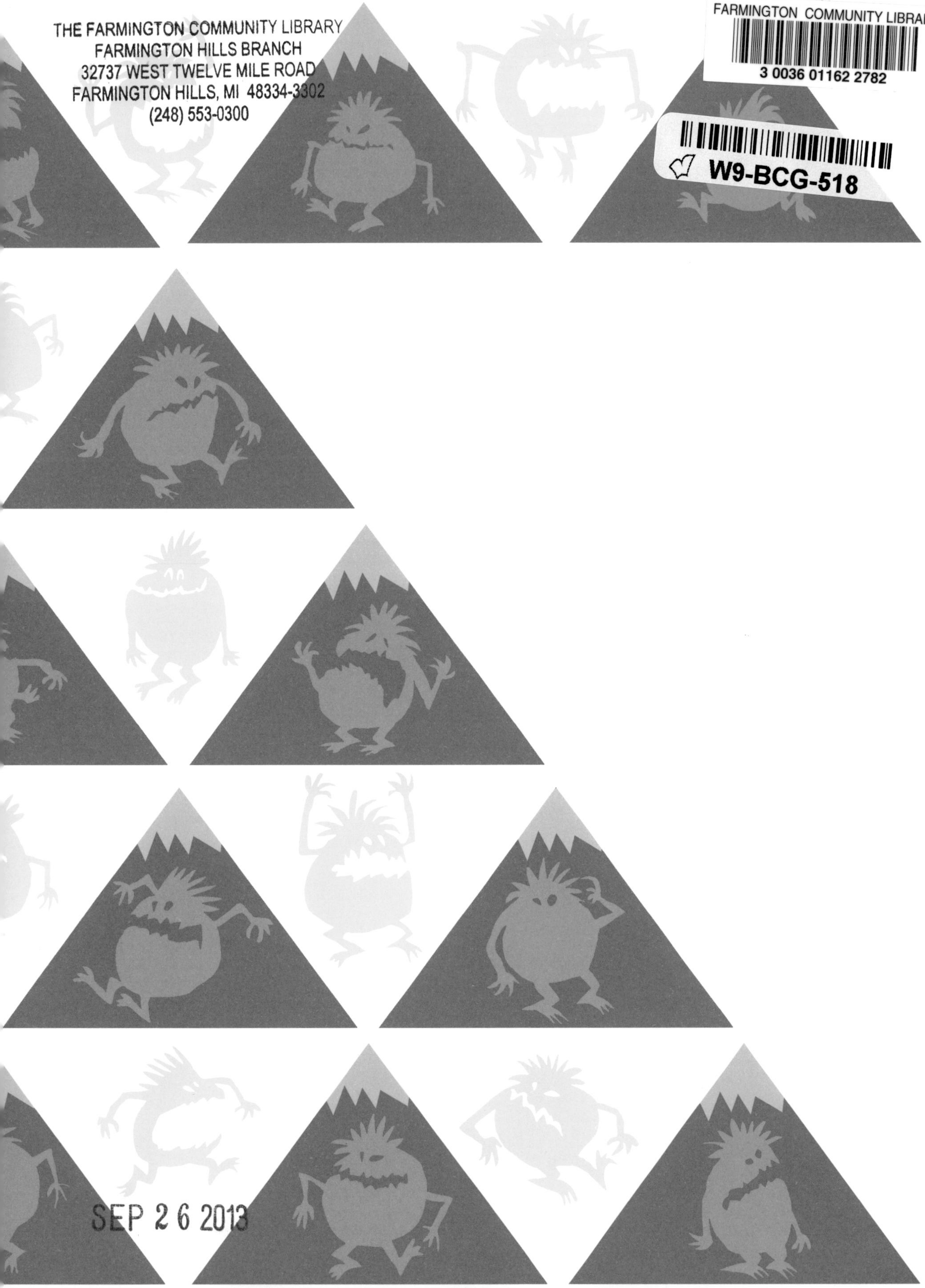

Lewis Trondheim

Monster Christmas

| Jean | Dad | Kriss | Petey | Mom |

PAPERCUTZ™

New York

IMPORTANT! READ THIS FIRST!

Petey and Jean love to draw pictures of monsters. One day they draw a scary monster that comes alive— it escapes right off the paper and disappears into their home! Well, they certainly have to do something about that, so they draw a nice monster, with three legs, four arms, and ten mouths to eat the bad monster. The plan works and Petey and Jean decide to keep the nice monster as a pet... and they name it Kriss.

Monster GRAPHIC NOVELS AVAILABLE FROM PAPERCUTZ ™

"Monster Christmas"

"Monster Mess"

COMING SOON:

"Monster Dinosaur"

Monster graphic novels from Papercutz are $9.99 in hardcover only, available at booksellers everywhere.

Or order from us: Please add $4.00 for postage and handling for the first book, add $1.00 for each additional book. Make check payable to NBM Publishing. Send to: Papercutz, 40 Exchange Place, Ste 1308, NY, NY 10005. (1-800-886-1223)

WWW.PAPERCUTZ.COM

MONSTER #1 "Monster Christmas"
Copyright © 1999 Guy Delcourt Productions
© 2011 Papercutz for the English Translation
All rights reserved.

Joe Johnson — Translation
Lea Hernandez — Lettering
Janice Chiang — Logo
Adam Grano — Production
Michael Petranek — Associate Editor
Jim Salicrup
Editor-in-Chief

ISBN: 978-1-59707-288-5

Printed in China
January 2012 by WKT Co. LTD.
3/F Phase I Leader Industrial Centre
188 Texaco Road, Tseun Wan, N.T., Hong Kong

DISTRIBUTED BY MACMILLAN
SECOND PAPERCUTZ PRINTING

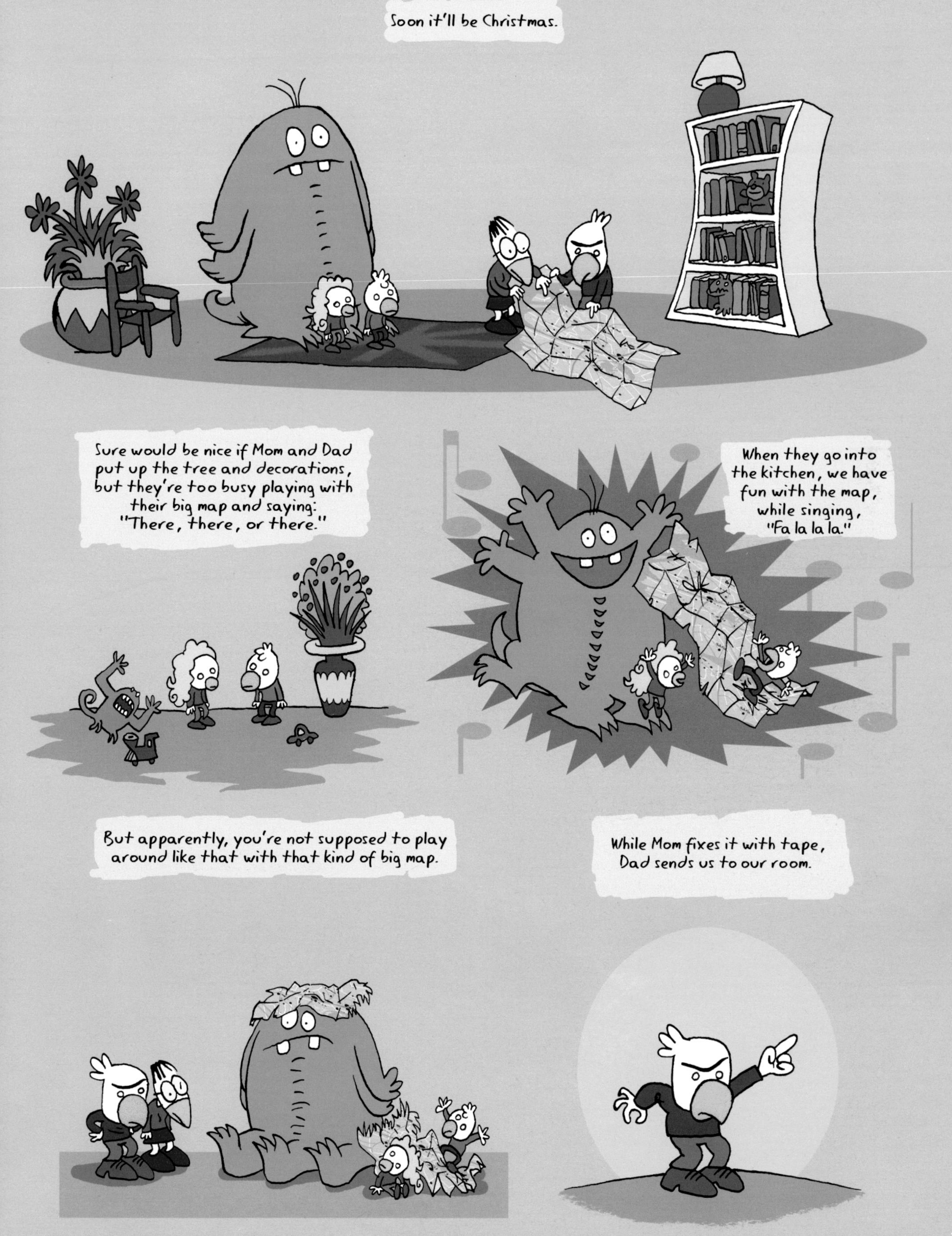
Soon it'll be Christmas.
Sure would be nice if Mom and Dad put up the tree and decorations, but they're too busy playing with their big map and saying: "There, there, or there."
When they go into the kitchen, we have fun with the map, while singing, "Fa la la la."
But apparently, you're not supposed to play around like that with that kind of big map.
While Mom fixes it with tape, Dad sends us to our room.

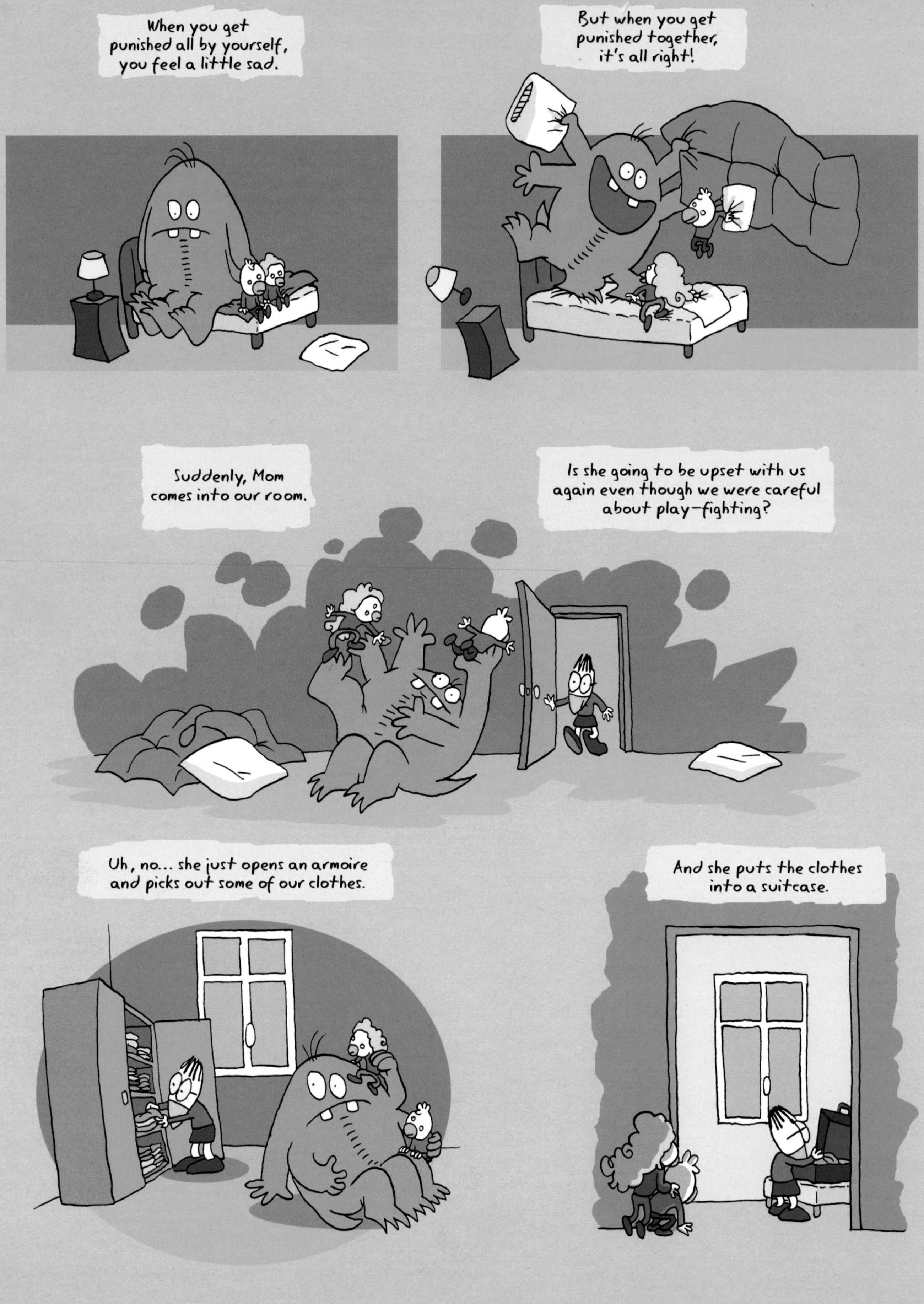
When you get punished all by yourself, you feel a little sad.
But when you get punished together, it's all right!
Suddenly, Mom comes into our room.
Is she going to be upset with us again even though we were careful about play-fighting?
Uh, no... she just opens an armoire and picks out some of our clothes.
And she puts the clothes into a suitcase.

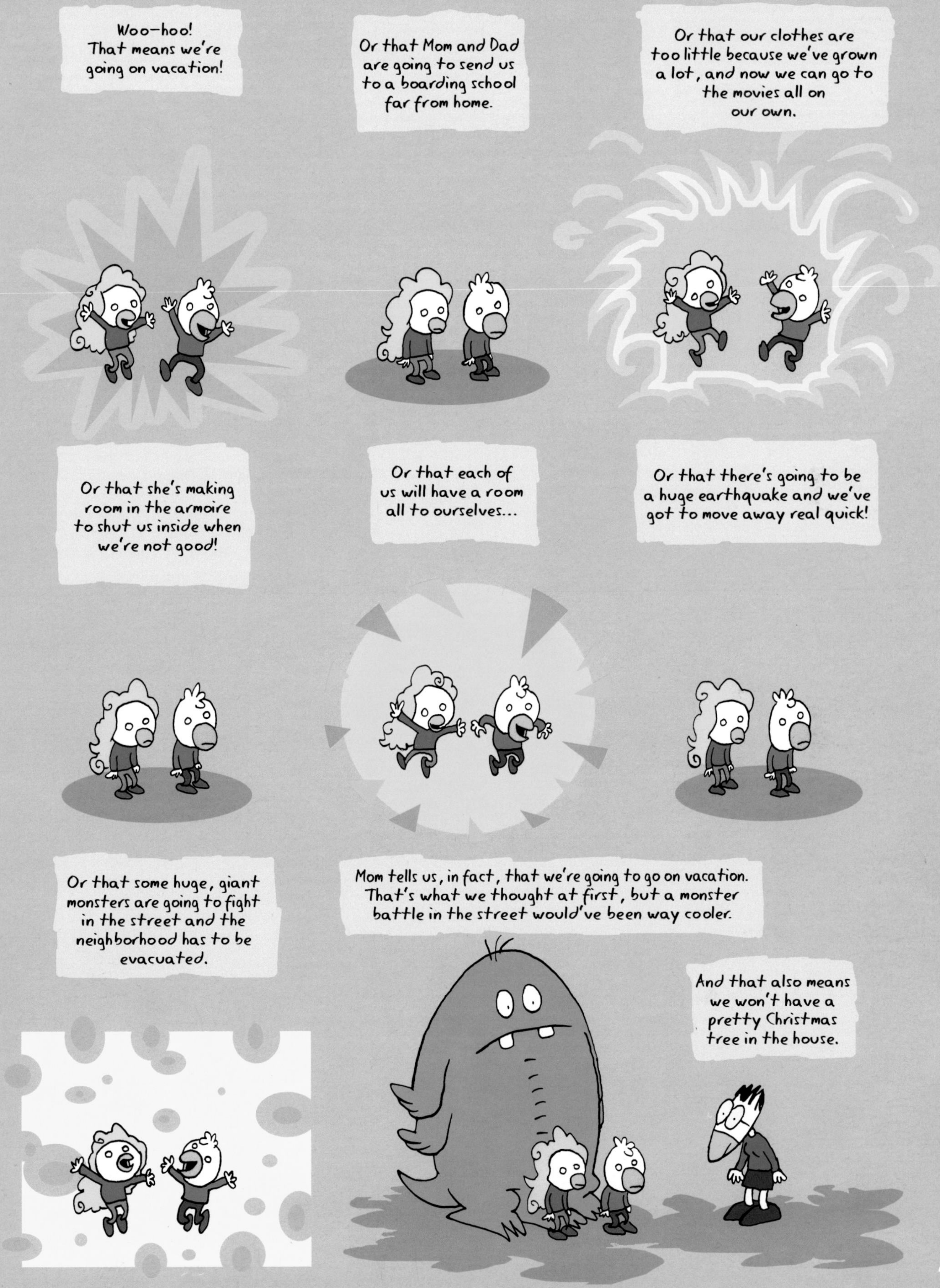
Woo-hoo! That means we're going on vacation!
Or that Mom and Dad are going to send us to a boarding school far from home.
Or that our clothes are too little because we've grown a lot, and now we can go to the movies all on our own.
Or that she's making room in the armoire to shut us inside when we're not good!
Or that each of us will have a room all to ourselves...
Or that there's going to be a huge earthquake and we've got to move away real quick!
Or that some huge, giant monsters are going to fight in the street and the neighborhood has to be evacuated.
Mom tells us, in fact, that we're going to go on vacation. That's what we thought at first, but a monster battle in the street would've been way cooler.
And that also means we won't have a pretty Christmas tree in the house.

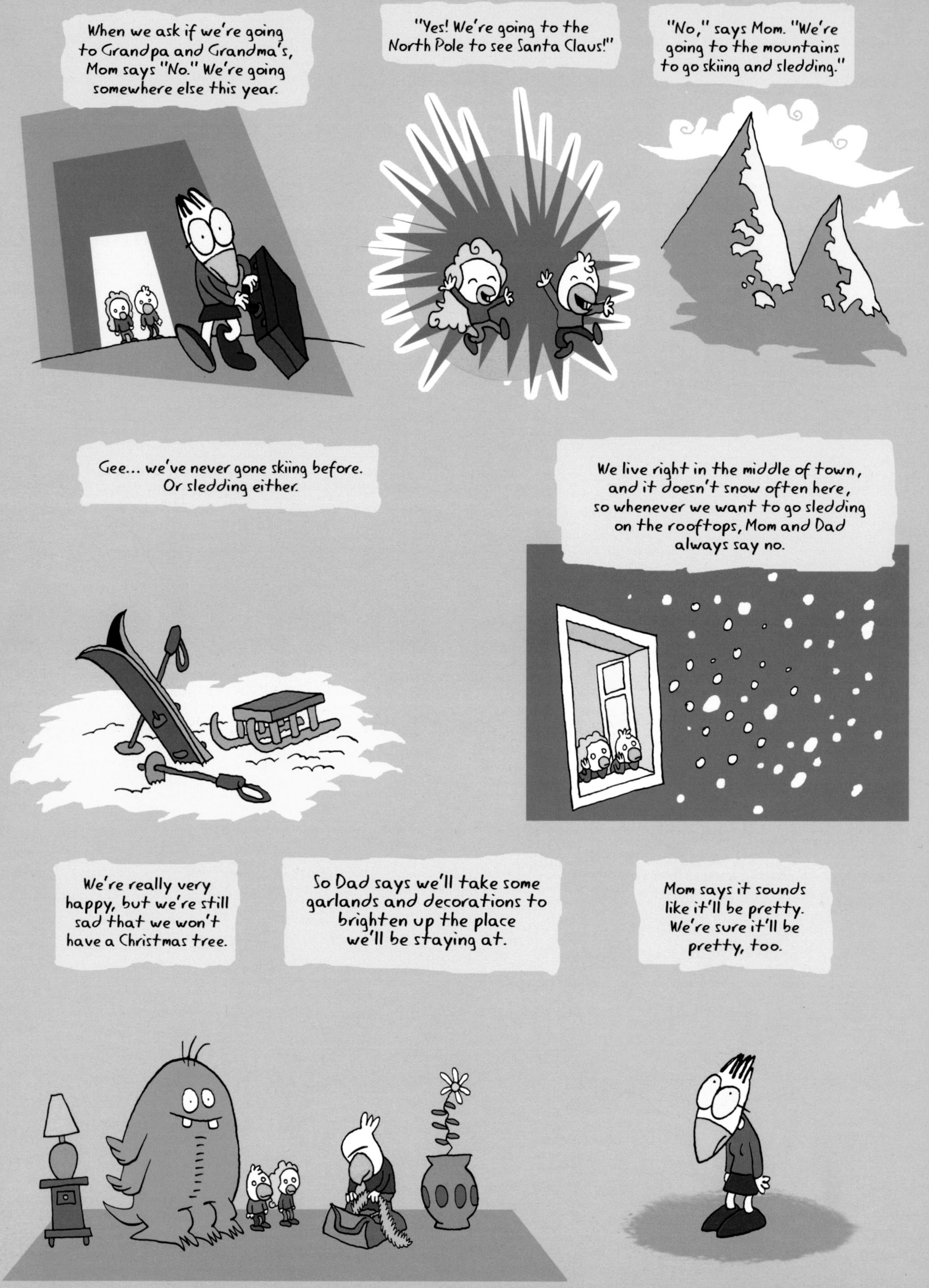
When we ask if we're going to Grandpa and Grandma's, Mom says "No." We're going somewhere else this year.
"Yes! We're going to the North Pole to see Santa Claus!"
"No," says Mom. "We're going to the mountains to go skiing and sledding."
Gee... we've never gone skiing before. Or sledding either.
We live right in the middle of town, and it doesn't snow often here, so whenever we want to go sledding on the rooftops, Mom and Dad always say no.
We're really very happy, but we're still sad that we won't have a Christmas tree.
So Dad says we'll take some garlands and decorations to brighten up the place we'll be staying at.
Mom says it sounds like it'll be pretty. We're sure it'll be pretty, too.

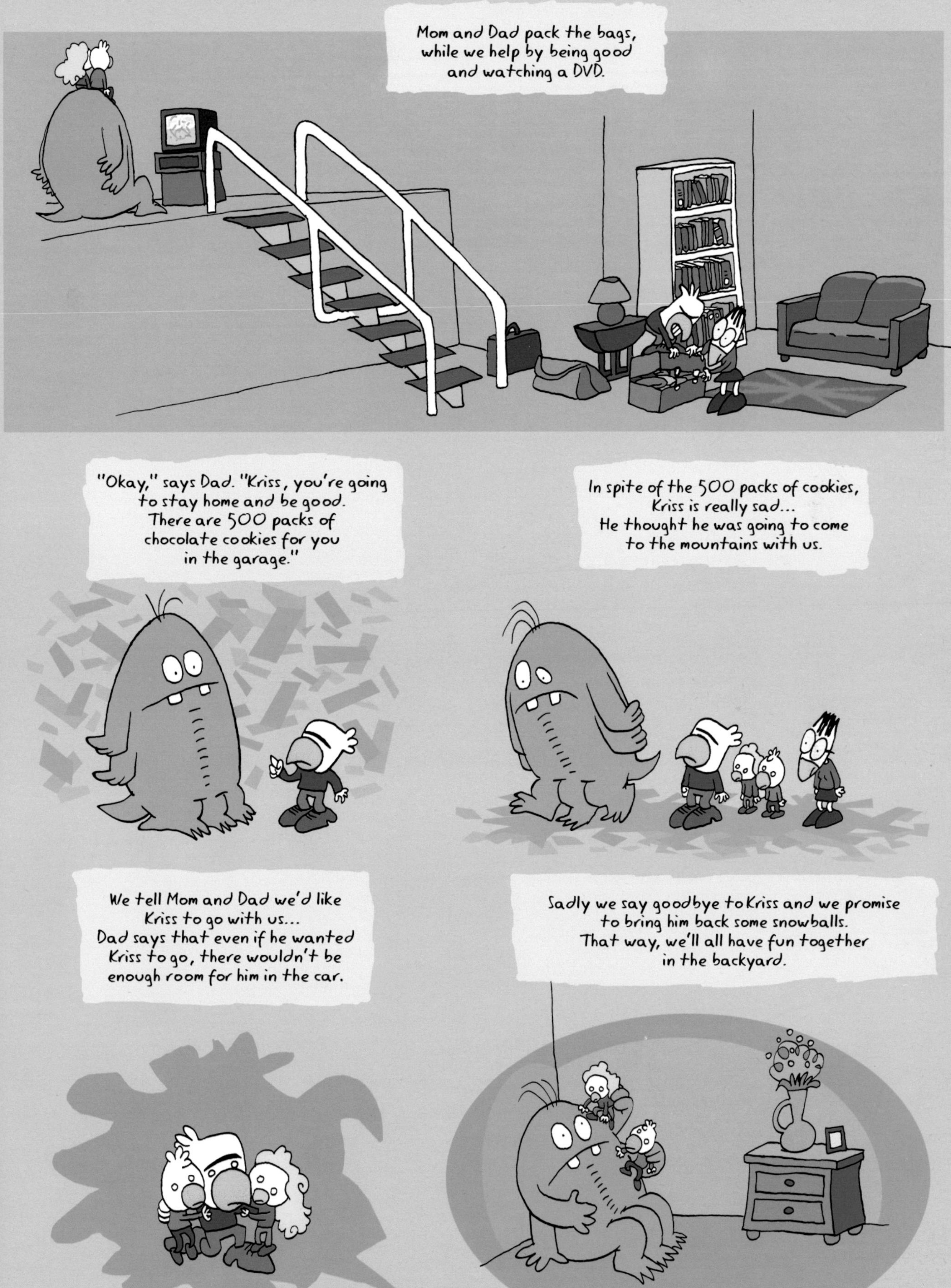
Mom and Dad pack the bags, while we help by being good and watching a DVD.
"Okay," says Dad. "Kriss, you're going to stay home and be good. There are 500 packs of chocolate cookies for you in the garage."
In spite of the 500 packs of cookies, Kriss is really sad... He thought he was going to come to the mountains with us.
We tell Mom and Dad we'd like Kriss to go with us... Dad says that even if he wanted Kriss to go, there wouldn't be enough room for him in the car.
Sadly we say goodbye to Kriss and we promise to bring him back some snowballs. That way, we'll all have fun together in the backyard.

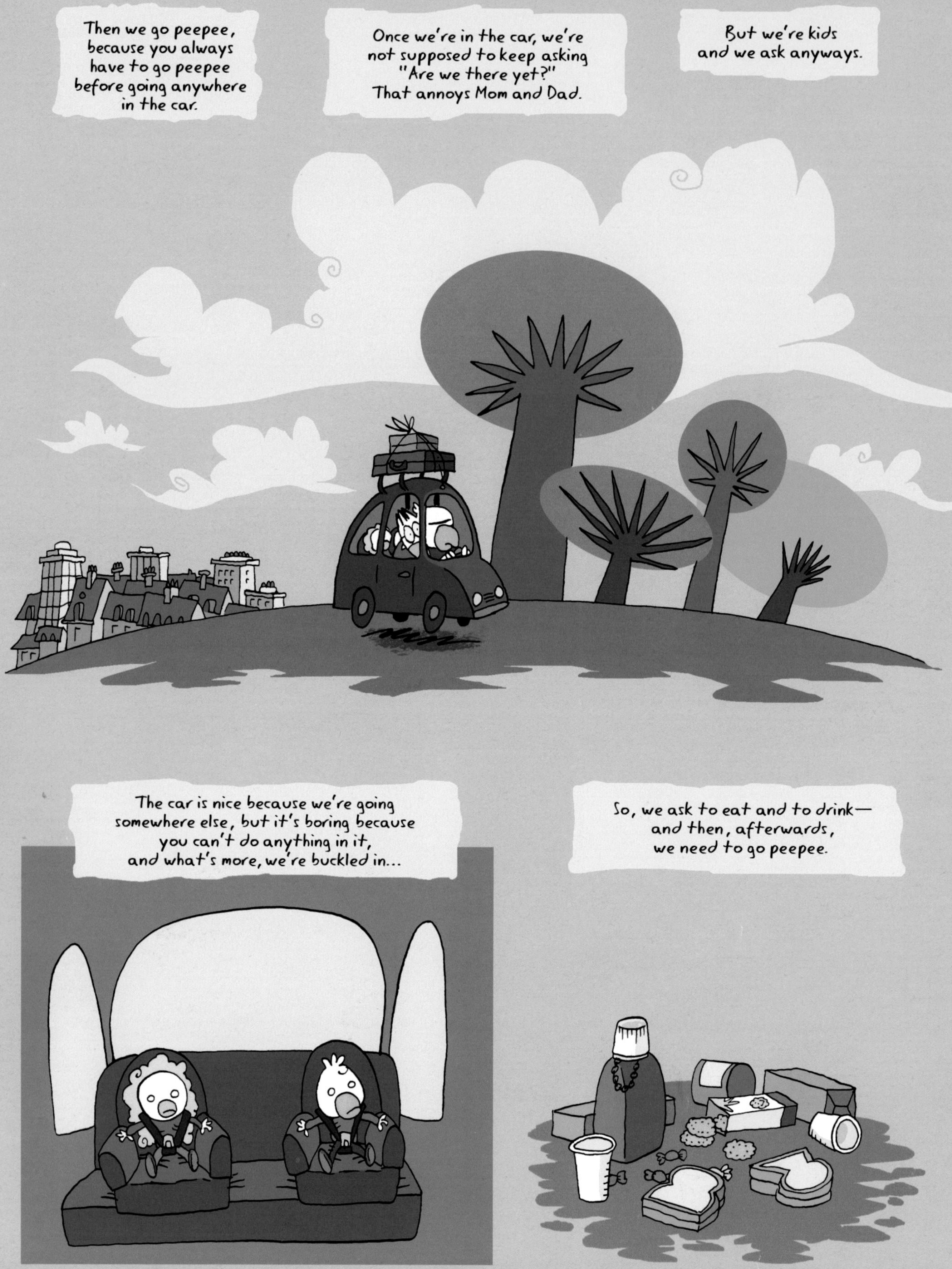
Then we go peepee, because you always have to go peepee before going anywhere in the car.
Once we're in the car, we're not supposed to keep asking "Are we there yet?" That annoys Mom and Dad.
But we're kids and we ask anyways.
The car is nice because we're going somewhere else, but it's boring because you can't do anything in it, and what's more, we're buckled in...
So, we ask to eat and to drink— and then, afterwards, we need to go peepee.

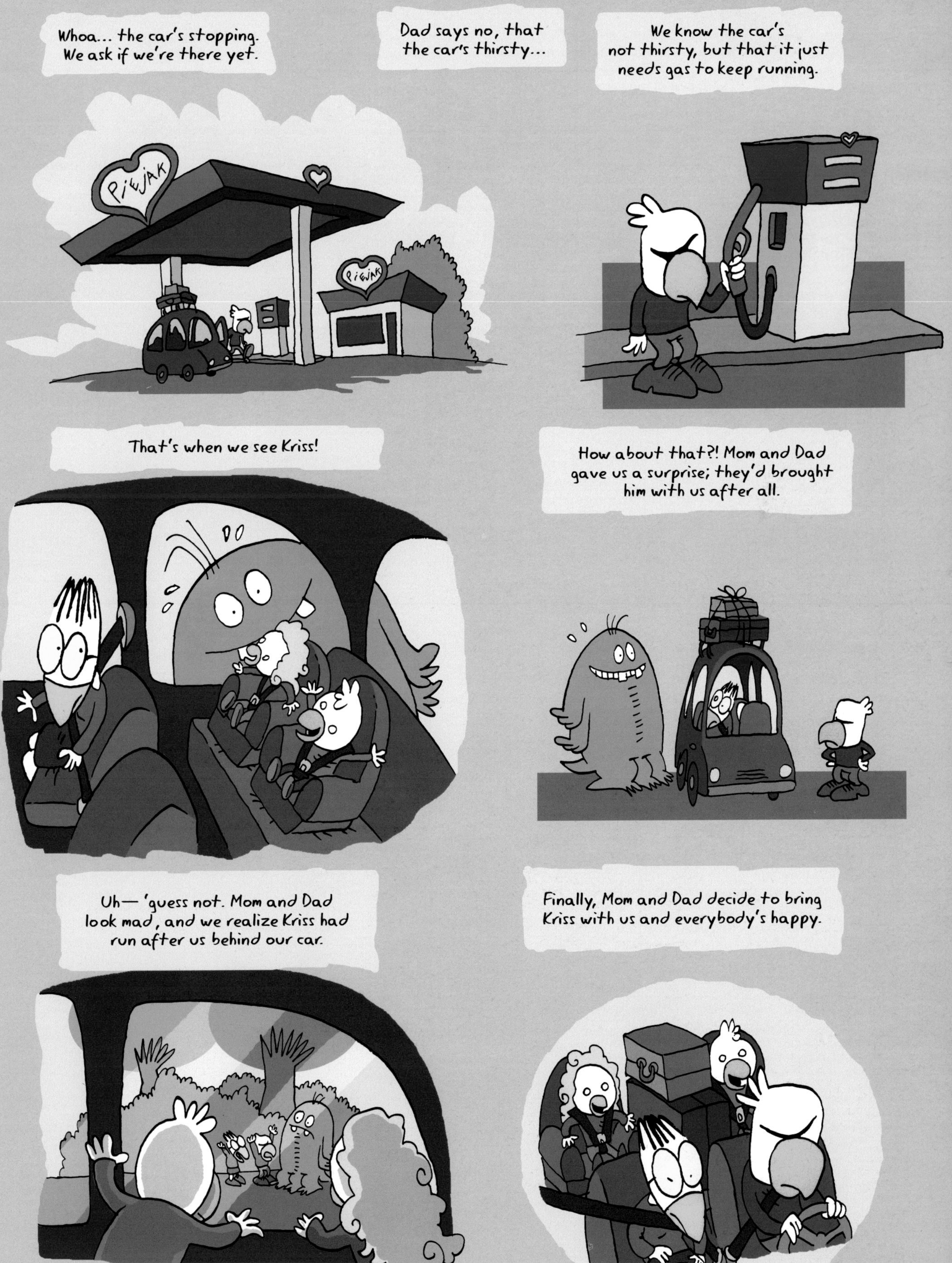
Whoa... the car's stopping. We ask if we're there yet.
Dad says no, that the car's thirsty...
We know the car's not thirsty, but that it just needs gas to keep running.
PIEJAK
That's when we see Kriss!
How about that?! Mom and Dad gave us a surprise; they'd brought him with us after all.
Uh— 'guess not. Mom and Dad look mad, and we realize Kriss had run after us behind our car.
Finally, Mom and Dad decide to bring Kriss with us and everybody's happy.

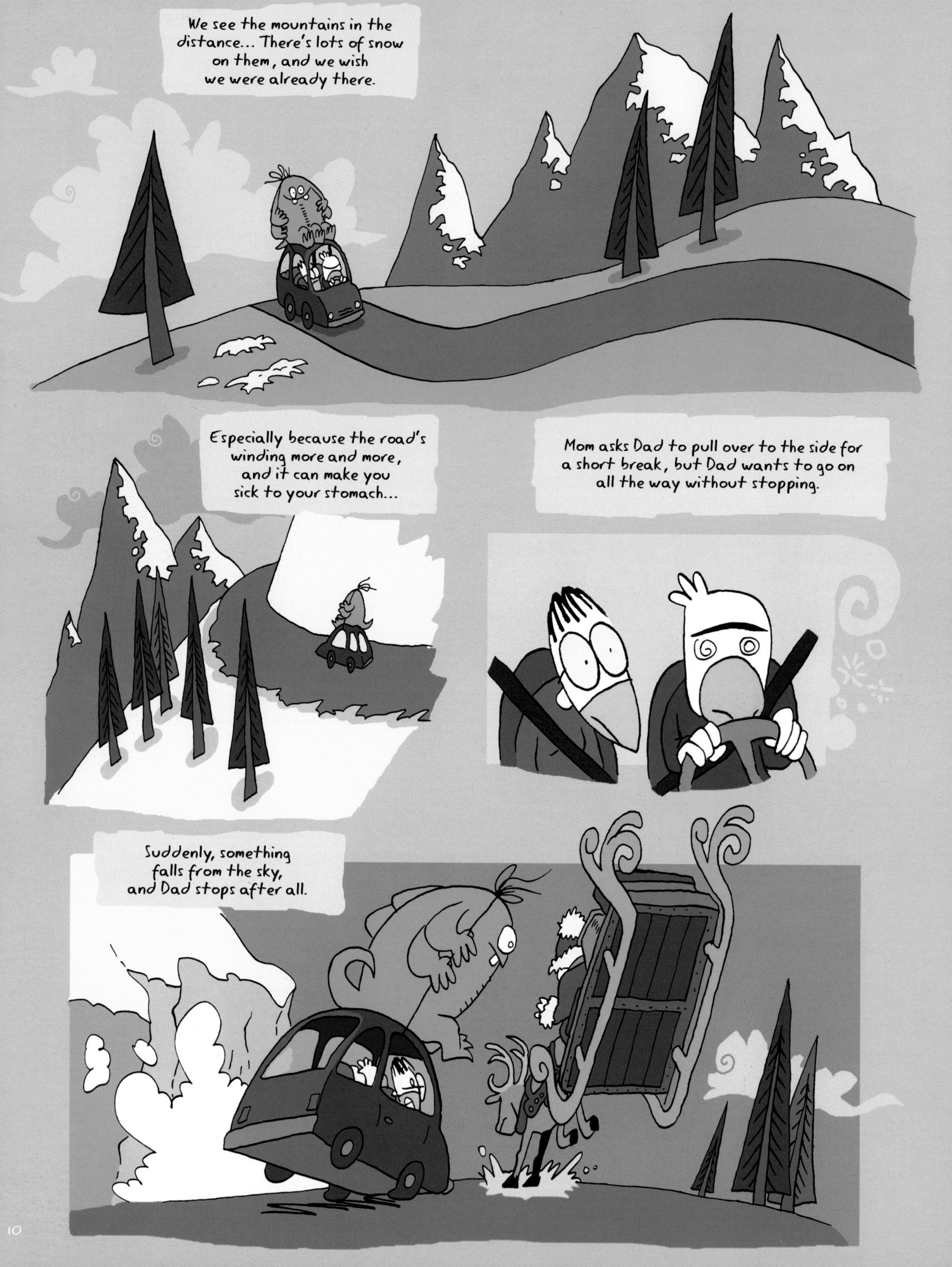

We see the mountains in the distance... There's lots of snow on them, and we wish we were already there.
Especially because the road's winding more and more, and it can make you sick to your stomach...
Mom asks Dad to pull over to the side for a short break, but Dad wants to go on all the way without stopping.
Suddenly, something falls from the sky, and Dad stops after all.

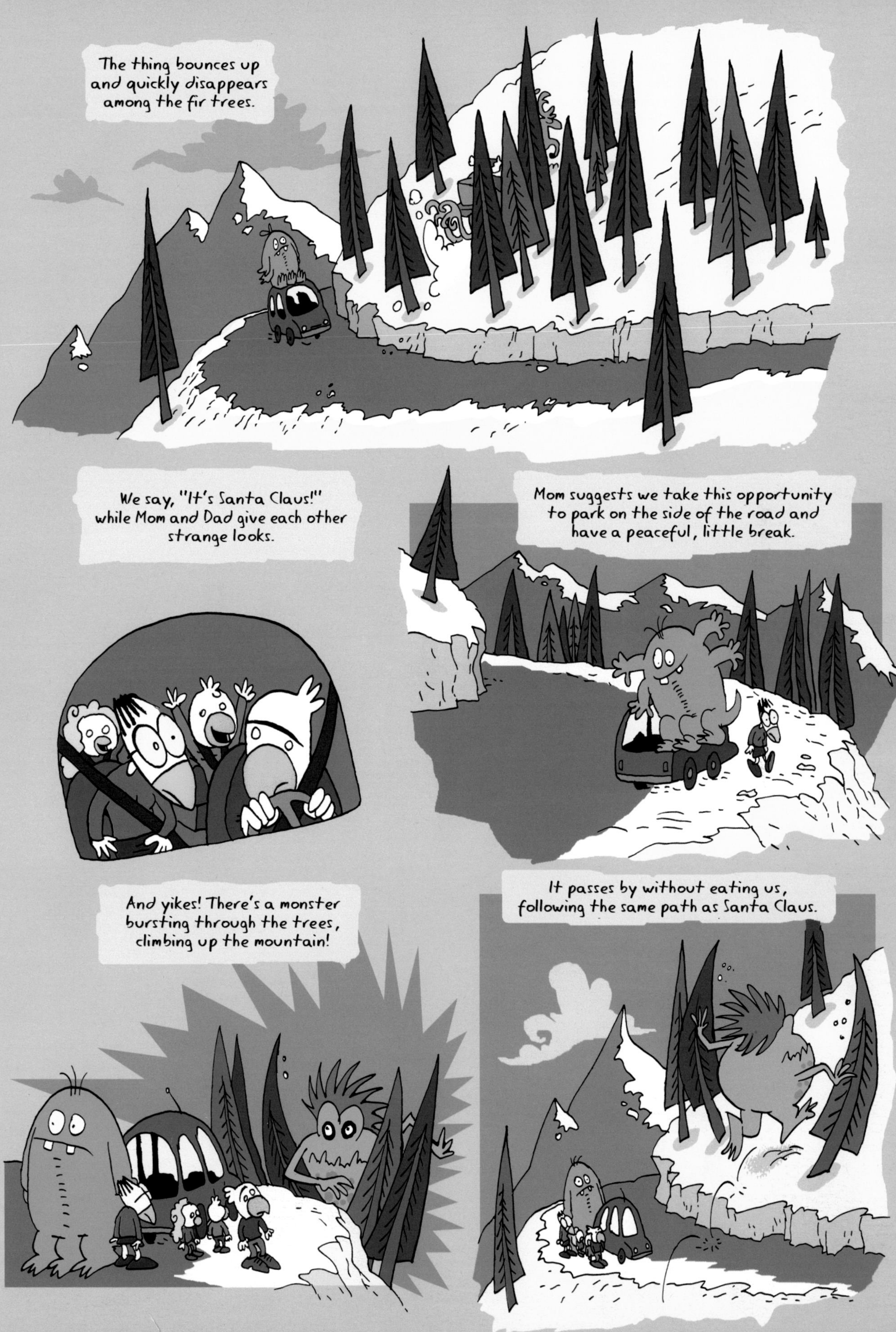
The thing bounces up and quickly disappears among the fir trees.
We say, "It's Santa Claus!" while Mom and Dad give each other strange looks.
Mom suggests we take this opportunity to park on the side of the road and have a peaceful, little break.
And yikes! There's a monster bursting through the trees, climbing up the mountain!
It passes by without eating us, following the same path as Santa Claus.

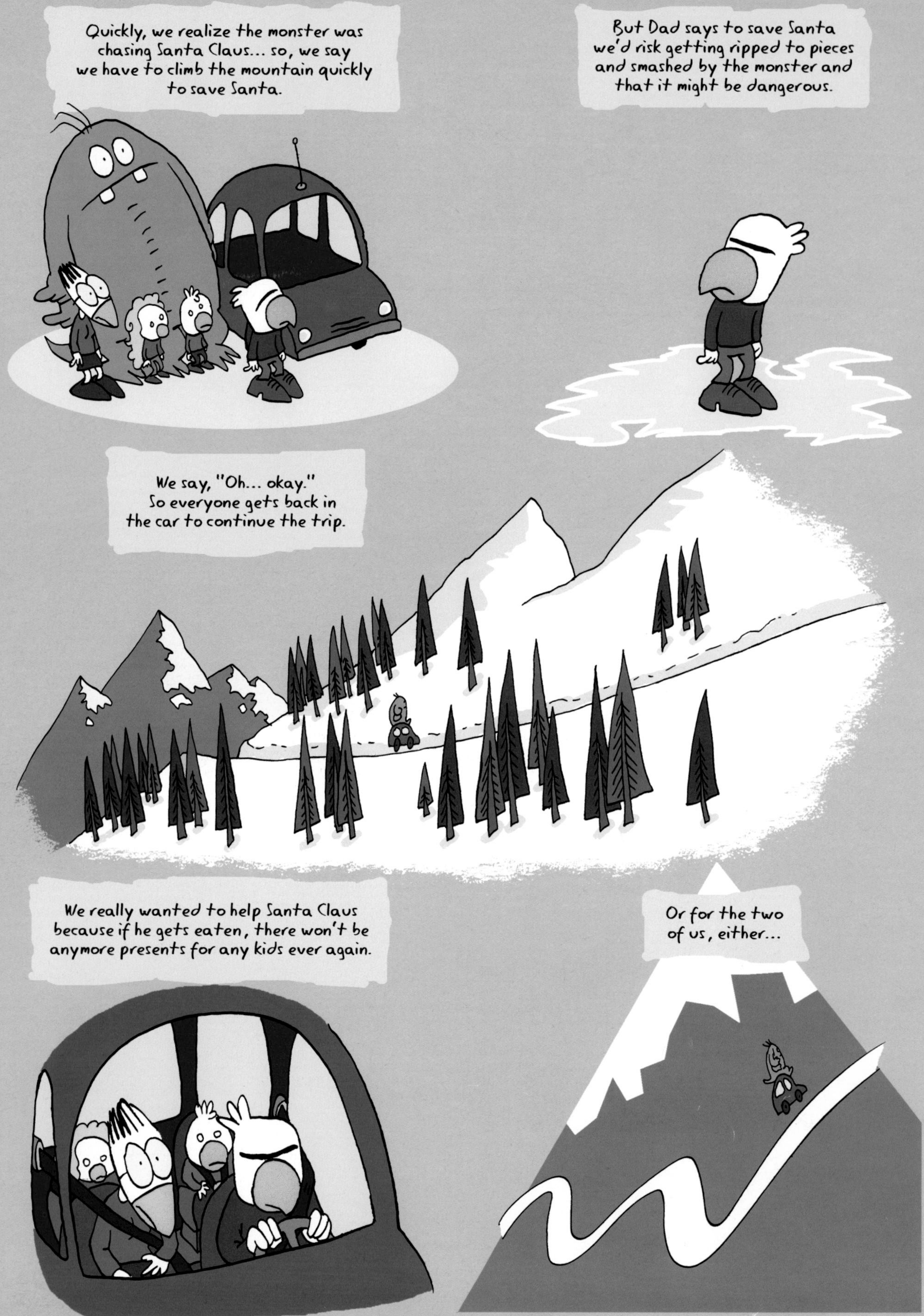
Quickly, we realize the monster was chasing Santa Claus... so, we say we have to climb the mountain quickly to save Santa.
But Dad says to save Santa we'd risk getting ripped to pieces and smashed by the monster and that it might be dangerous.
We say, "Oh... okay." So everyone gets back in the car to continue the trip.
We really wanted to help Santa Claus because if he gets eaten, there won't be anymore presents for any kids ever again.
Or for the two of us, either...

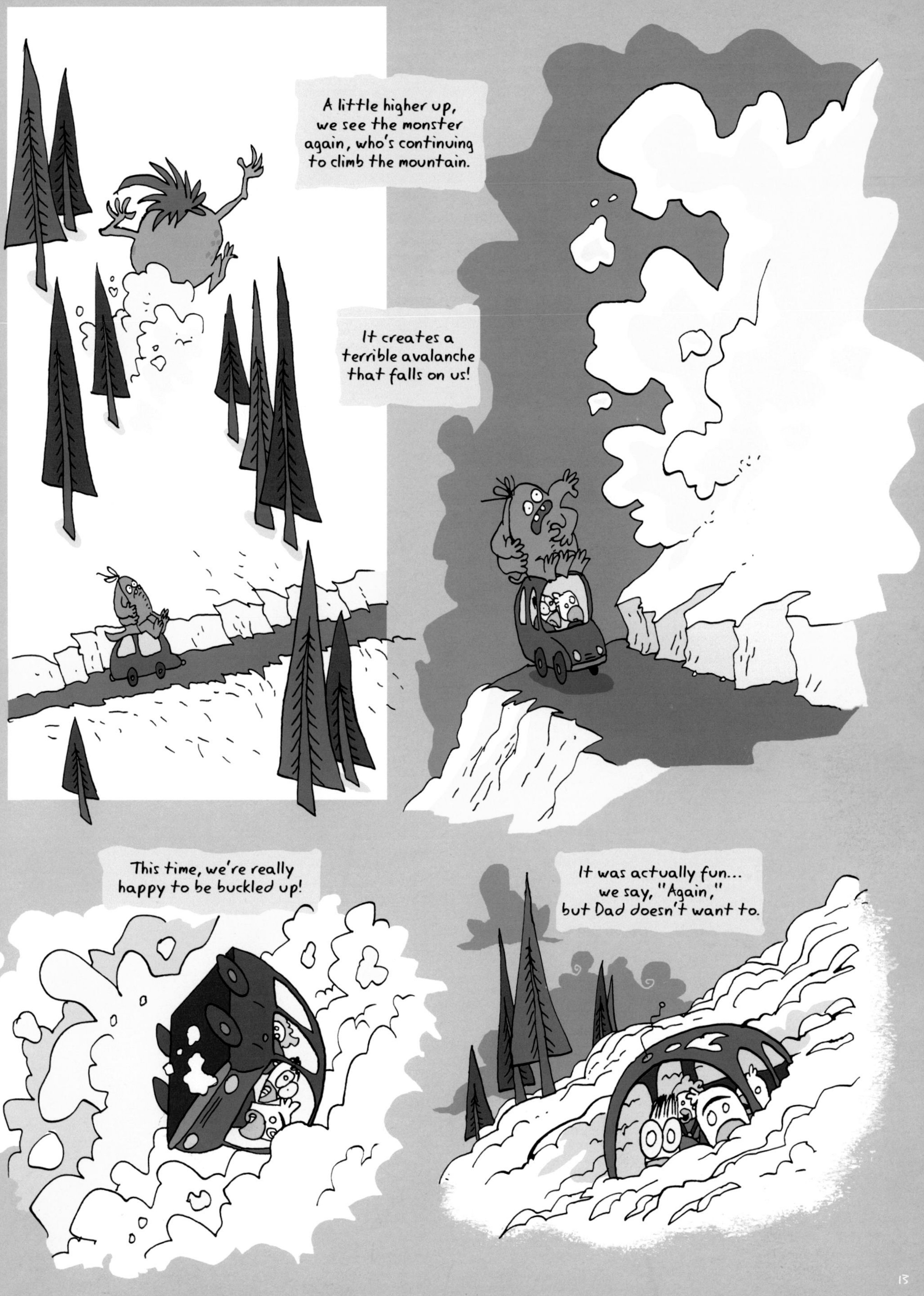
A little higher up, we see the monster again, who's continuing to climb the mountain.
It creates a terrible avalanche that falls on us!
This time, we're really happy to be buckled up!
It was actually fun... we say, "Again," but Dad doesn't want to.

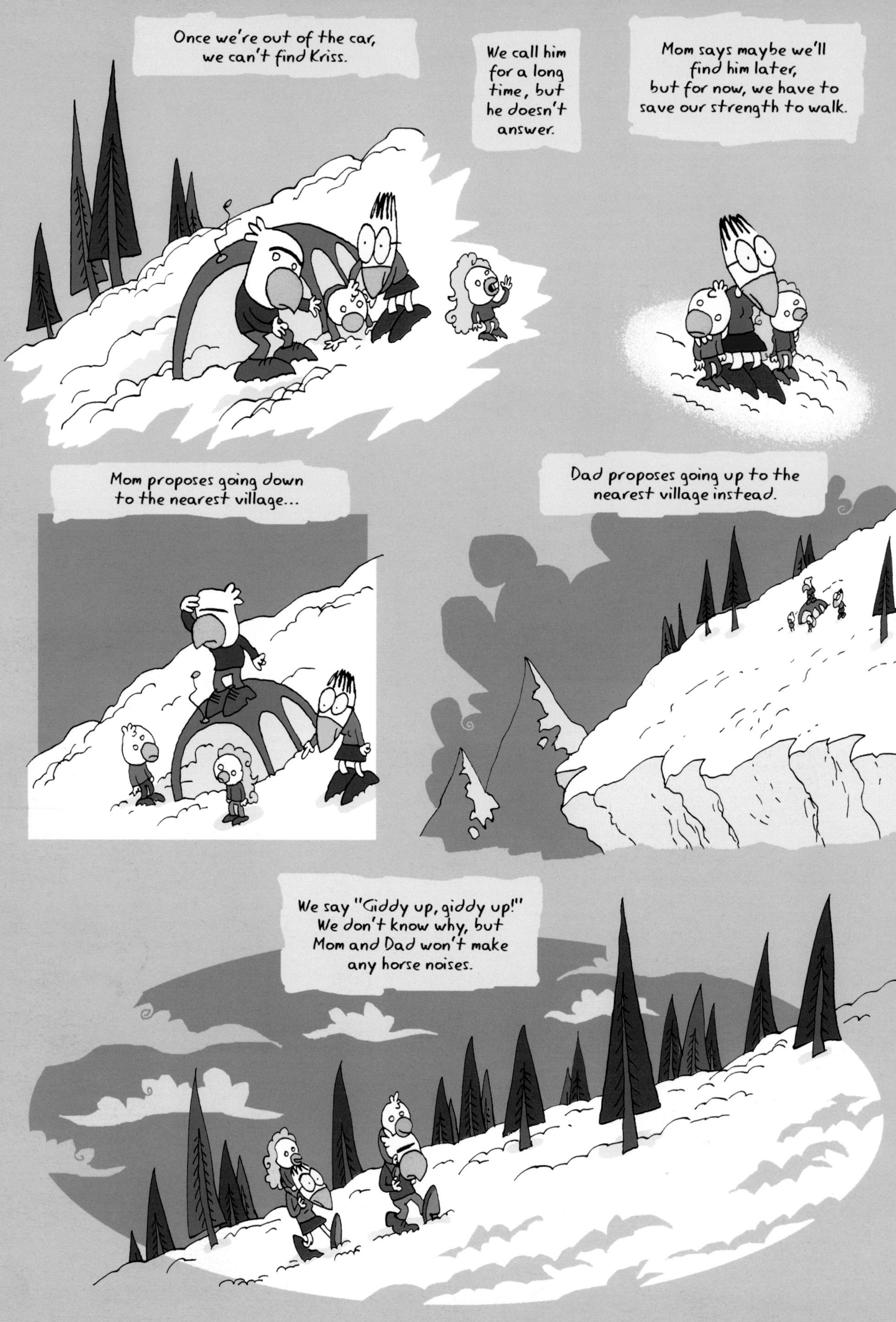
Once we're out of the car, we can't find Kriss.
We call him for a long time, but he doesn't answer.
Mom says maybe we'll find him later, but for now, we have to save our strength to walk.
Mom proposes going down to the nearest village...
Dad proposes going up to the nearest village instead.
We say "Giddy up, giddy up!" We don't know why, but Mom and Dad won't make any horse noises.

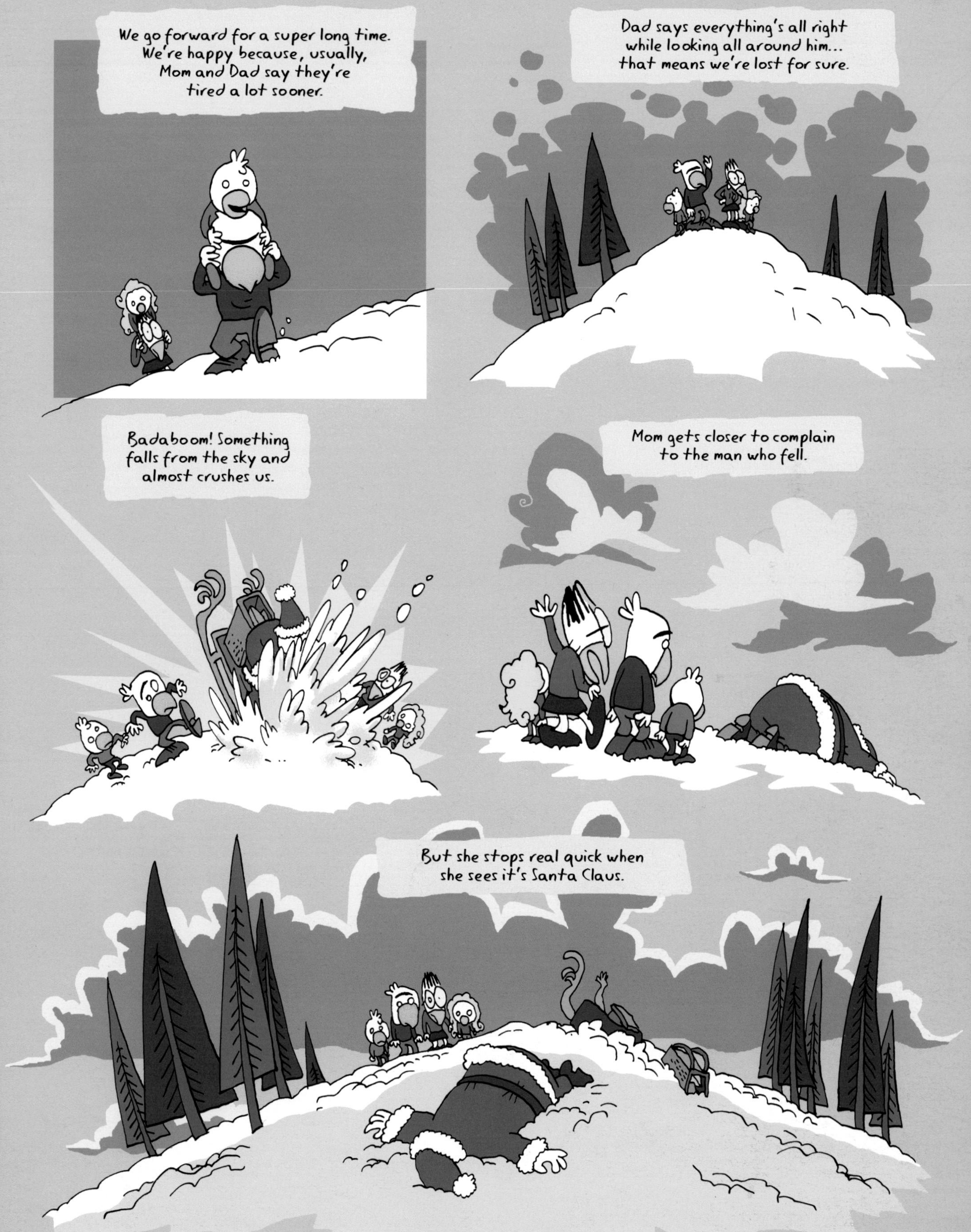
We go forward for a super long time. We're happy because, usually, Mom and Dad say they're tired a lot sooner.
Dad says everything's all right while looking all around him... that means we're lost for sure.
Badaboom! Something falls from the sky and almost crushes us.
Mom gets closer to complain to the man who fell.
But she stops real quick when she sees it's Santa Claus.

We quickly go to help him.

We don't need any bandages or mercurochrome to wake him up, some hugs and kisses are enough.

At first Santa is happy, but a little later he tells us to leave quickly.

When we ask why, he says it's because of the big monster that's chasing him.

It ate all of the sleigh's reindeer, and Santa doesn't want any harm to come to us, too.

Right then, we hear a loud noise coming toward us, and the fir trees separate as an enormous creature passes through!

Santa tells us to get behind him.

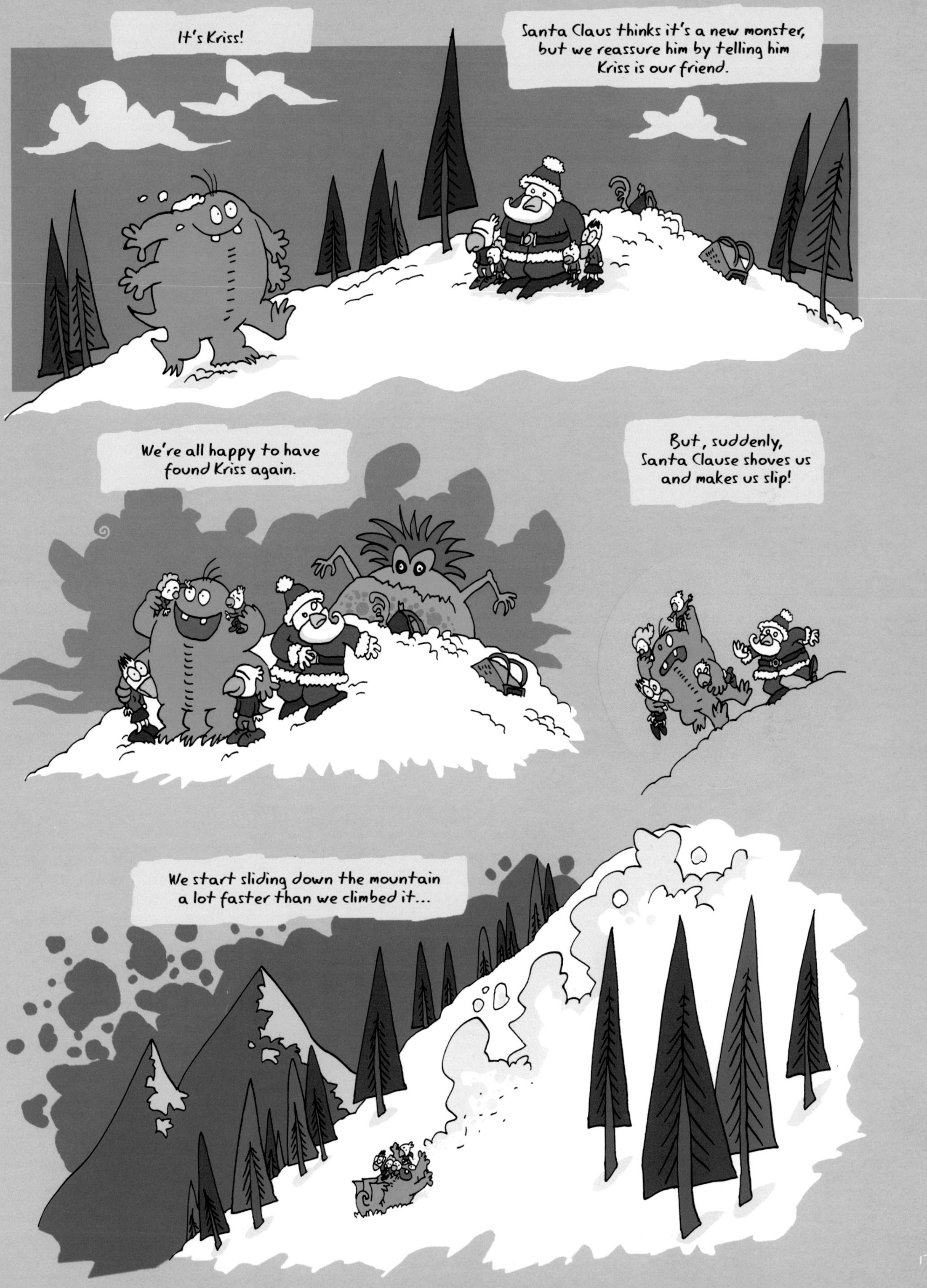
It's Kriss!
Santa Claus thinks it's a new monster, but we reassure him by telling him Kriss is our friend.
We're all happy to have found Kriss again.
But, suddenly, Santa Clause shoves us and makes us slip!
We start sliding down the mountain a lot faster than we climbed it...

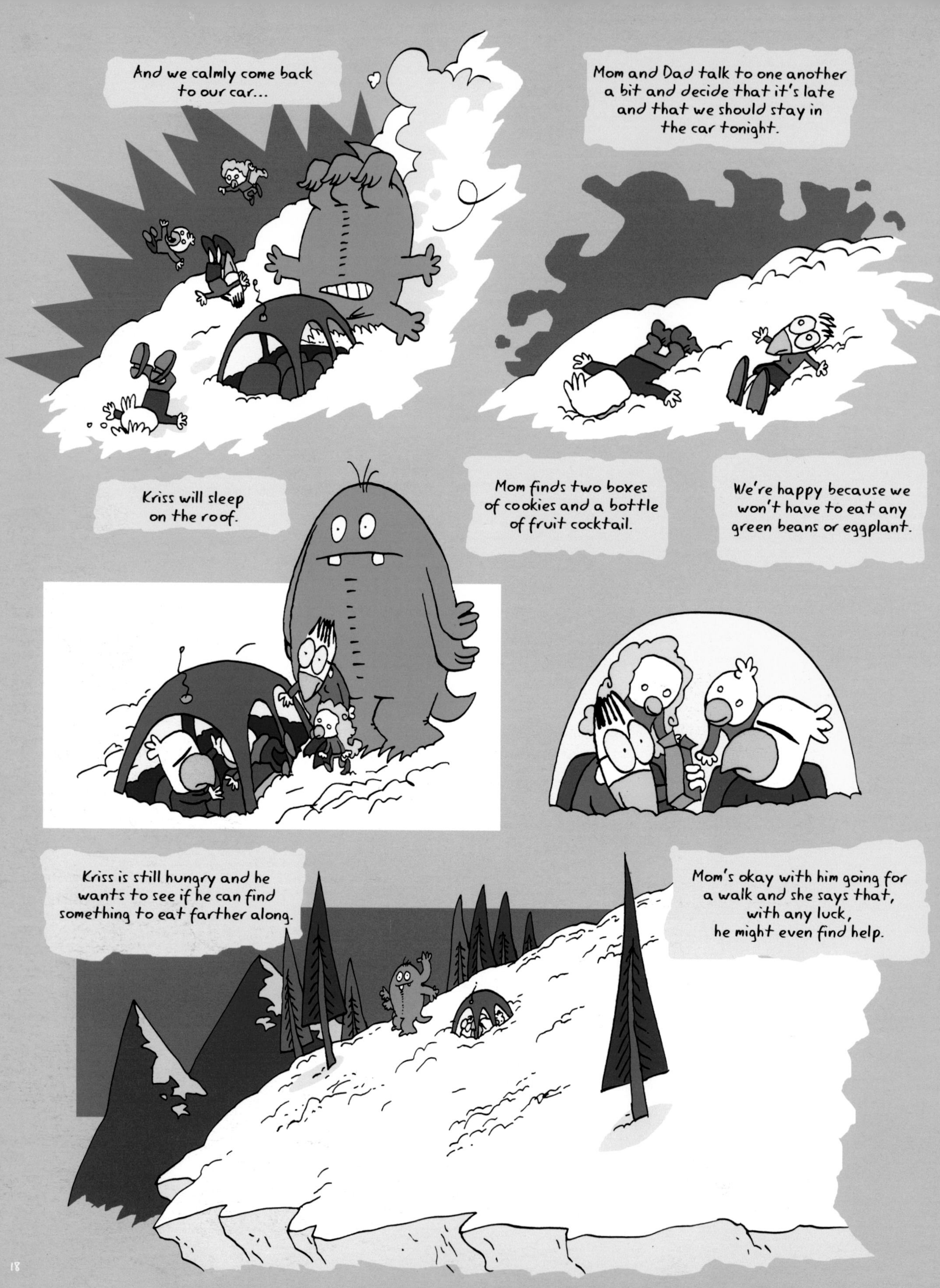
And we calmly come back to our car...
Mom and Dad talk to one another a bit and decide that it's late and that we should stay in the car tonight.
Kriss will sleep on the roof.
Mom finds two boxes of cookies and a bottle of fruit cocktail.
We're happy because we won't have to eat any green beans or eggplant.
Kriss is still hungry and he wants to see if he can find something to eat farther along.
Mom's okay with him going for a walk and she says that, with any luck, he might even find help.

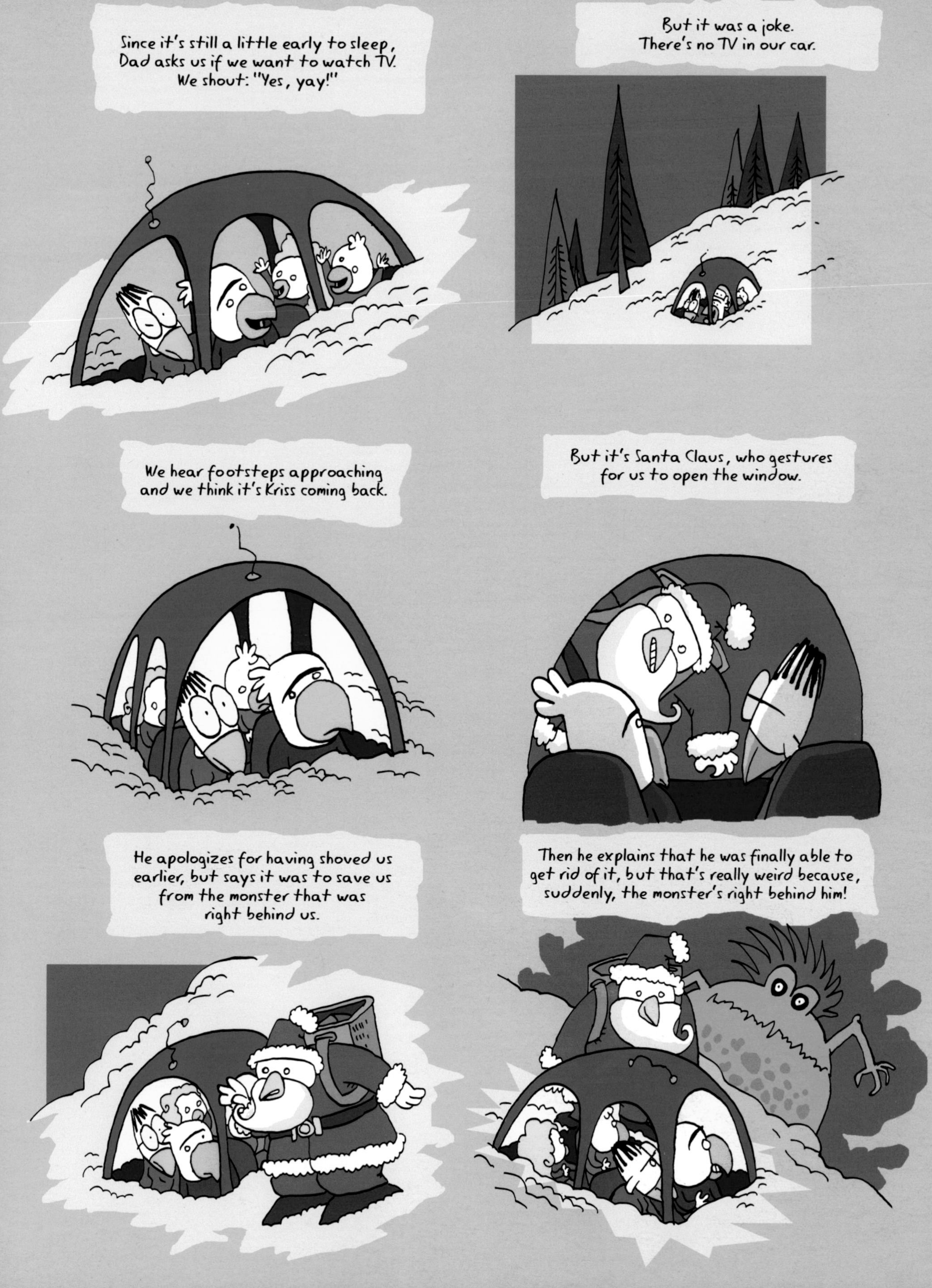
Since it's still a little early to sleep, Dad asks us if we want to watch TV. We shout: "Yes, yay!"
But it was a joke. There's no TV in our car.
We hear footsteps approaching and we think it's Kriss coming back.
But it's Santa Claus, who gestures for us to open the window.
He apologizes for having shoved us earlier, but says it was to save us from the monster that was right behind us.
Then he explains that he was finally able to get rid of it, but that's really weird because, suddenly, the monster's right behind him!

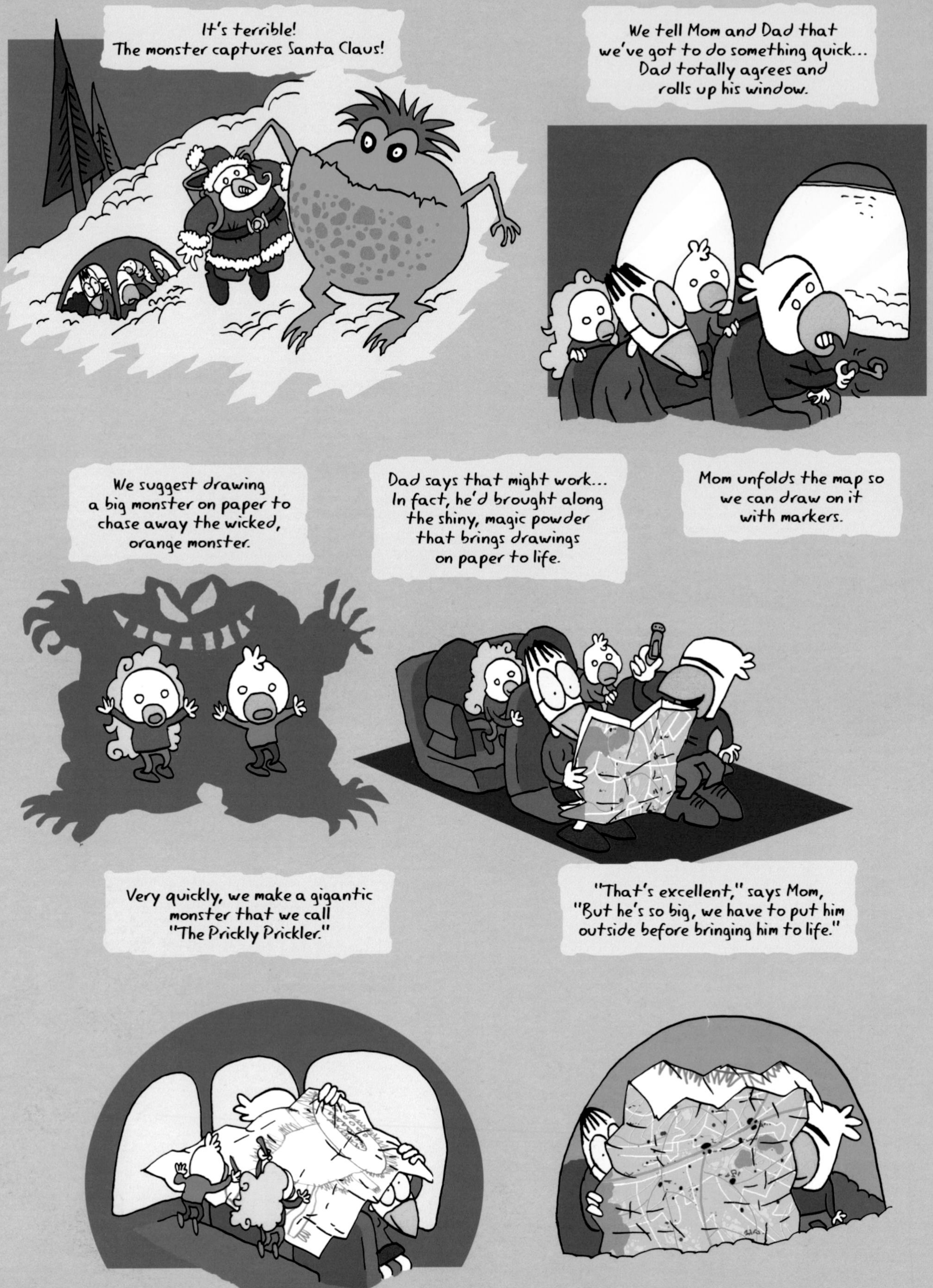
It's terrible!
The monster captures Santa Claus!
We tell Mom and Dad that we've got to do something quick... Dad totally agrees and rolls up his window.
We suggest drawing a big monster on paper to chase away the wicked, orange monster.
Dad says that might work... In fact, he'd brought along the shiny, magic powder that brings drawings on paper to life.
Mom unfolds the map so we can draw on it with markers.
Very quickly, we make a gigantic monster that we call "The Prickly Prickler."
"That's excellent," says Mom, "But he's so big, we have to put him outside before bringing him to life."

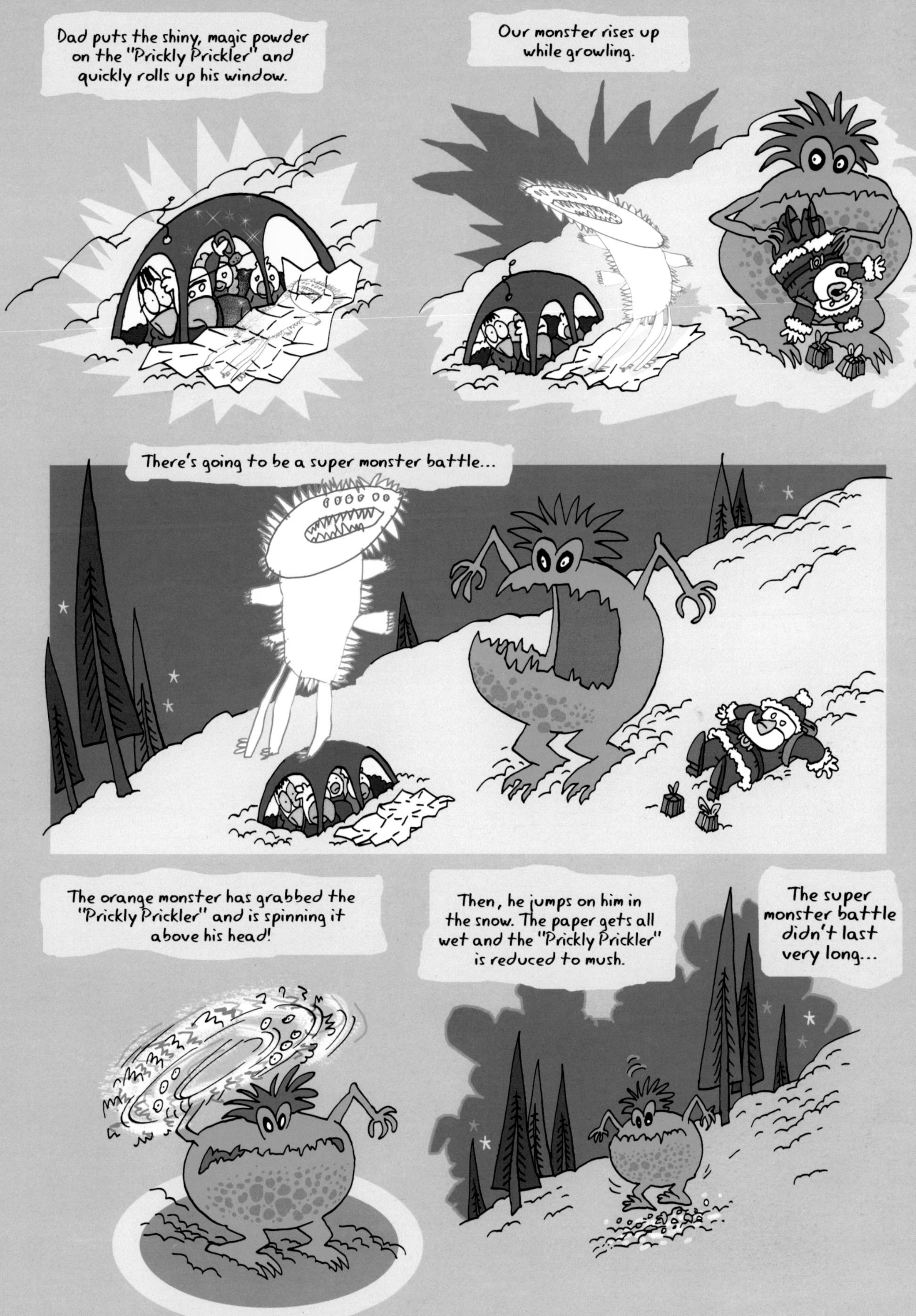
Dad puts the shiny, magic powder on the "Prickly Prickler" and quickly rolls up his window.
Our monster rises up while growling.
There's going to be a super monster battle...
The orange monster has grabbed the "Prickly Prickler" and is spinning it above his head!
Then, he jumps on him in the snow. The paper gets all wet and the "Prickly Prickler" is reduced to mush.
The super monster battle didn't last very long...

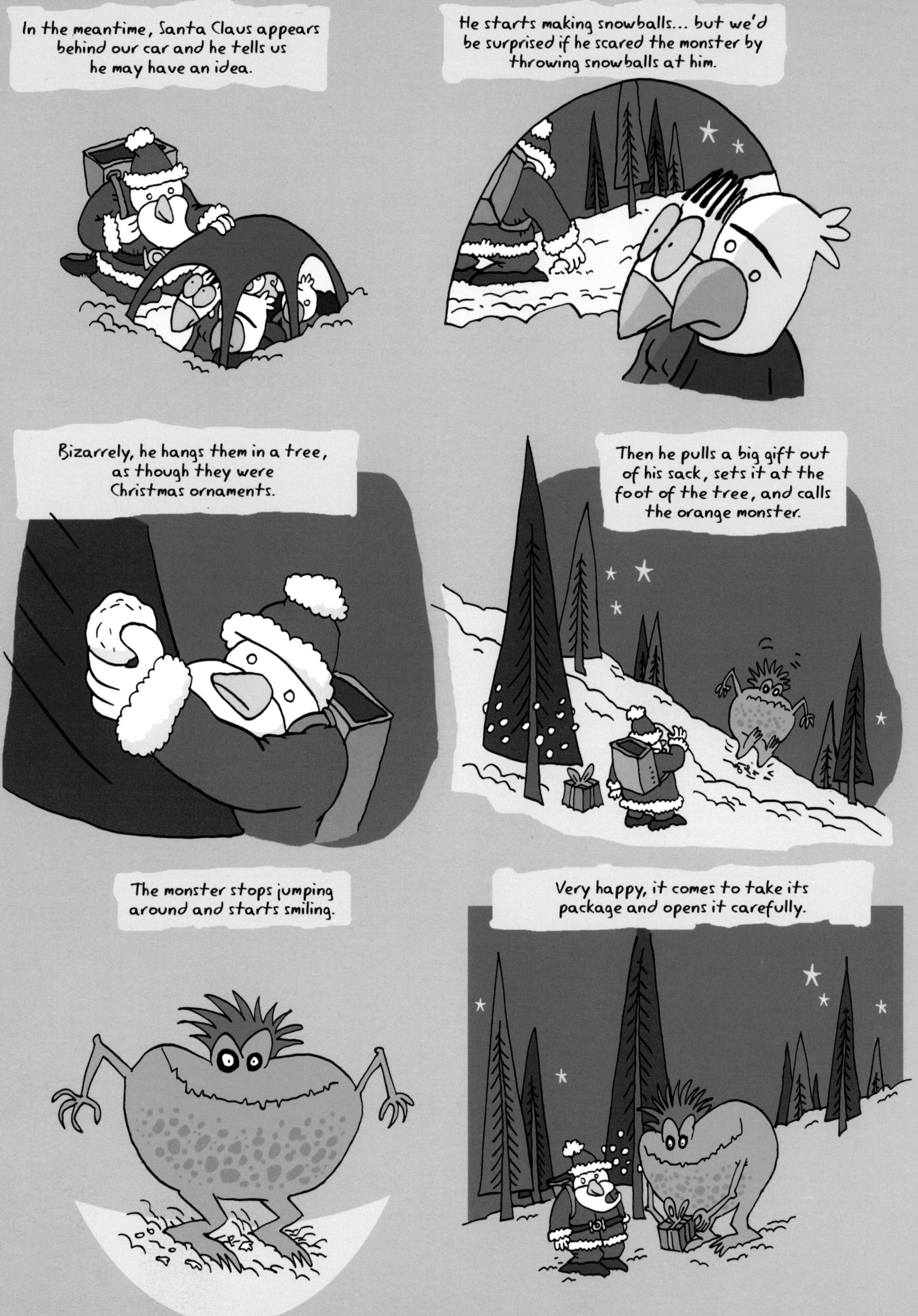
In the meantime, Santa Claus appears behind our car and he tells us he may have an idea.
He starts making snowballs... but we'd be surprised if he scared the monster by throwing snowballs at him.
Bizarrely, he hangs them in a tree, as though they were Christmas ornaments.
Then he pulls a big gift out of his sack, sets it at the foot of the tree, and calls the orange monster.
The monster stops jumping around and starts smiling.
Very happy, it comes to take its package and opens it carefully.

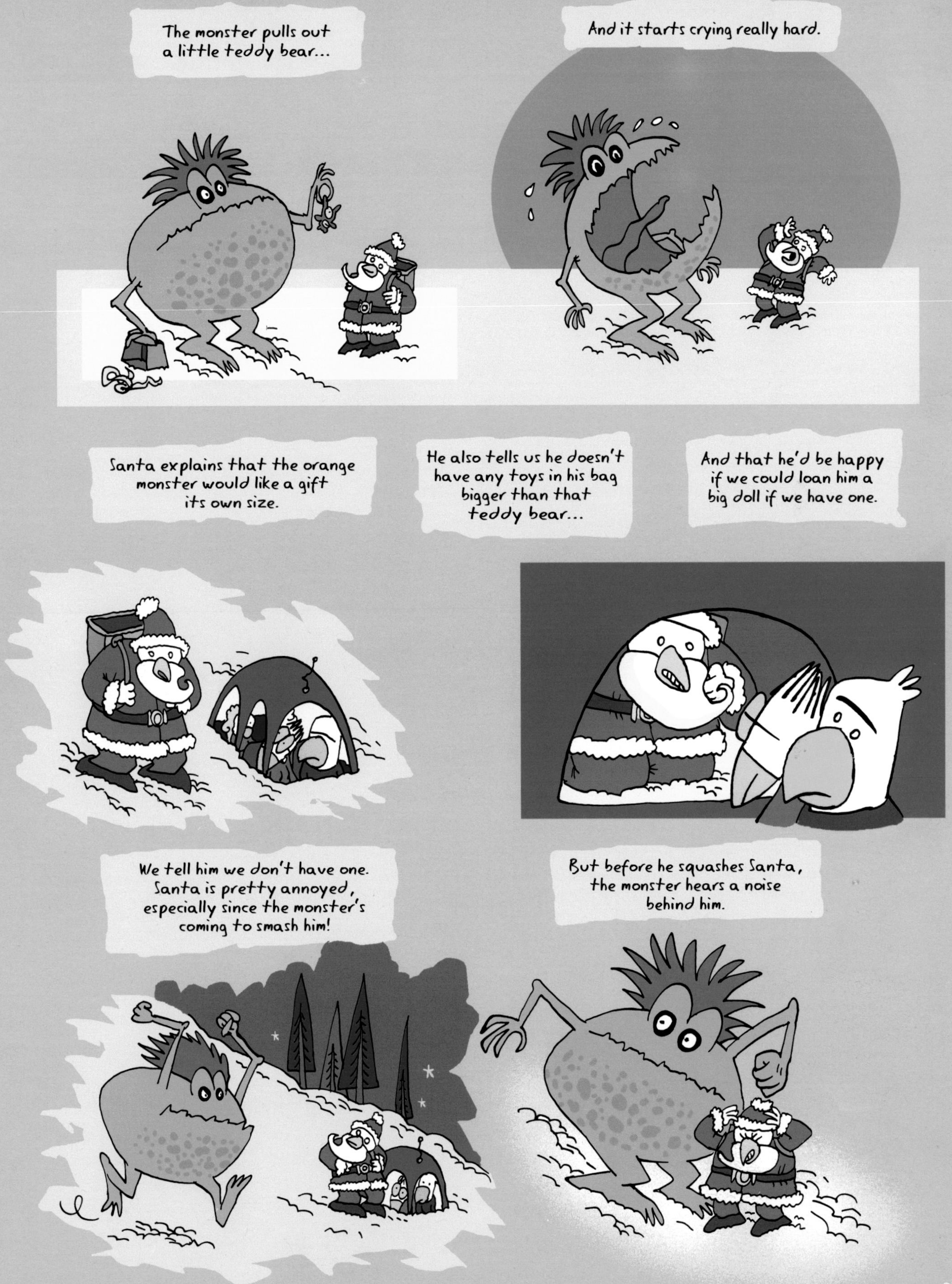
The monster pulls out a little teddy bear...
And it starts crying really hard.
Santa explains that the orange monster would like a gift its own size.
He also tells us he doesn't have any toys in his bag bigger than that teddy bear...
And that he'd be happy if we could loan him a big doll if we have one.
We tell him we don't have one. Santa is pretty annoyed, especially since the monster's coming to smash him!
But before he squashes Santa, the monster hears a noise behind him.

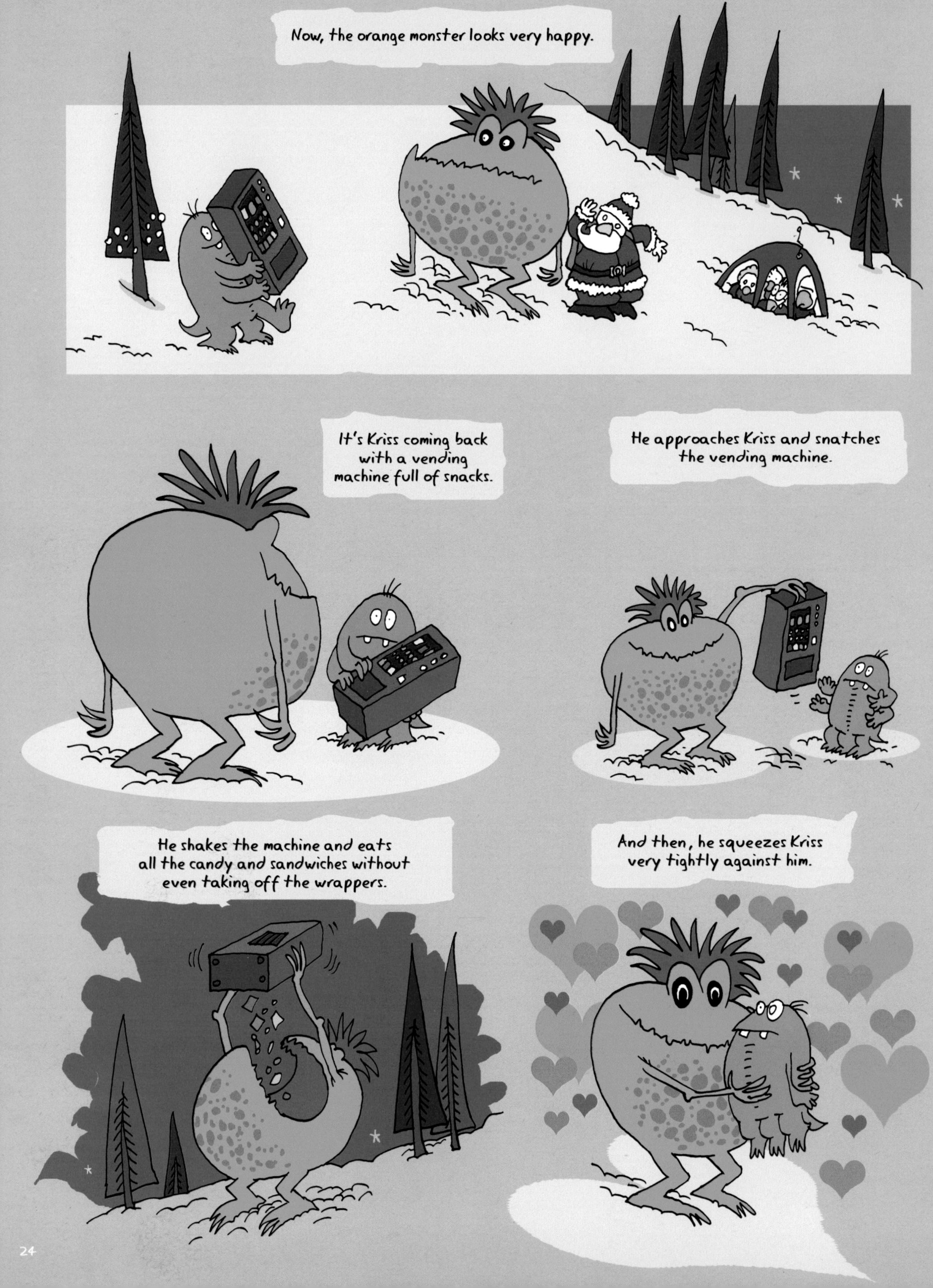
Now, the orange monster looks very happy.
It's Kriss coming back with a vending machine full of snacks.
He approaches Kriss and snatches the vending machine.
He shakes the machine and eats all the candy and sandwiches without even taking off the wrappers.
And then, he squeezes Kriss very tightly against him.

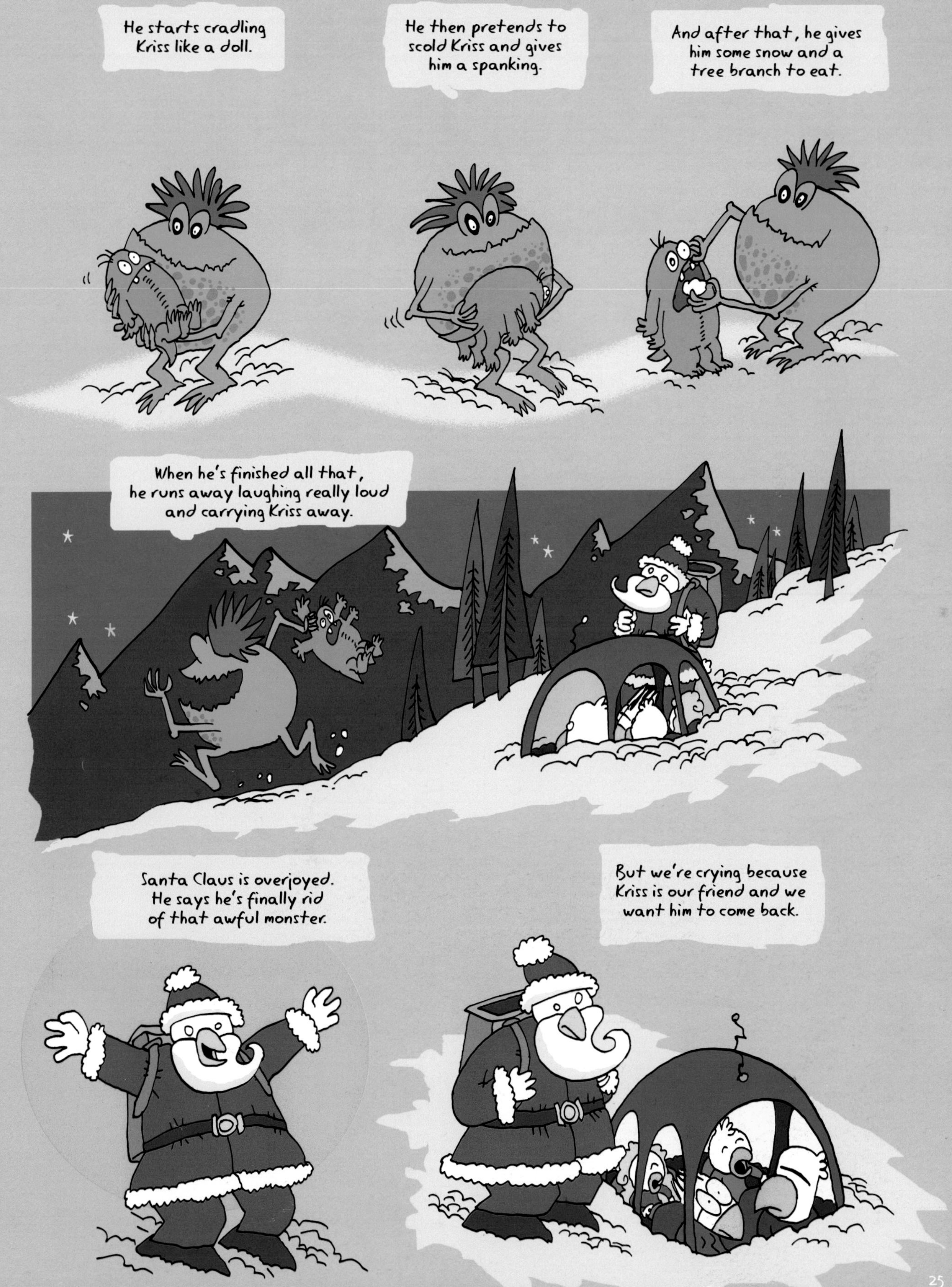
He starts cradling Kriss like a doll.
He then pretends to scold Kriss and gives him a spanking.
And after that, he gives him some snow and a tree branch to eat.
When he's finished all that, he runs away laughing really loud and carrying Kriss away.
Santa Claus is overjoyed. He says he's finally rid of that awful monster.
But we're crying because Kriss is our friend and we want him to come back.

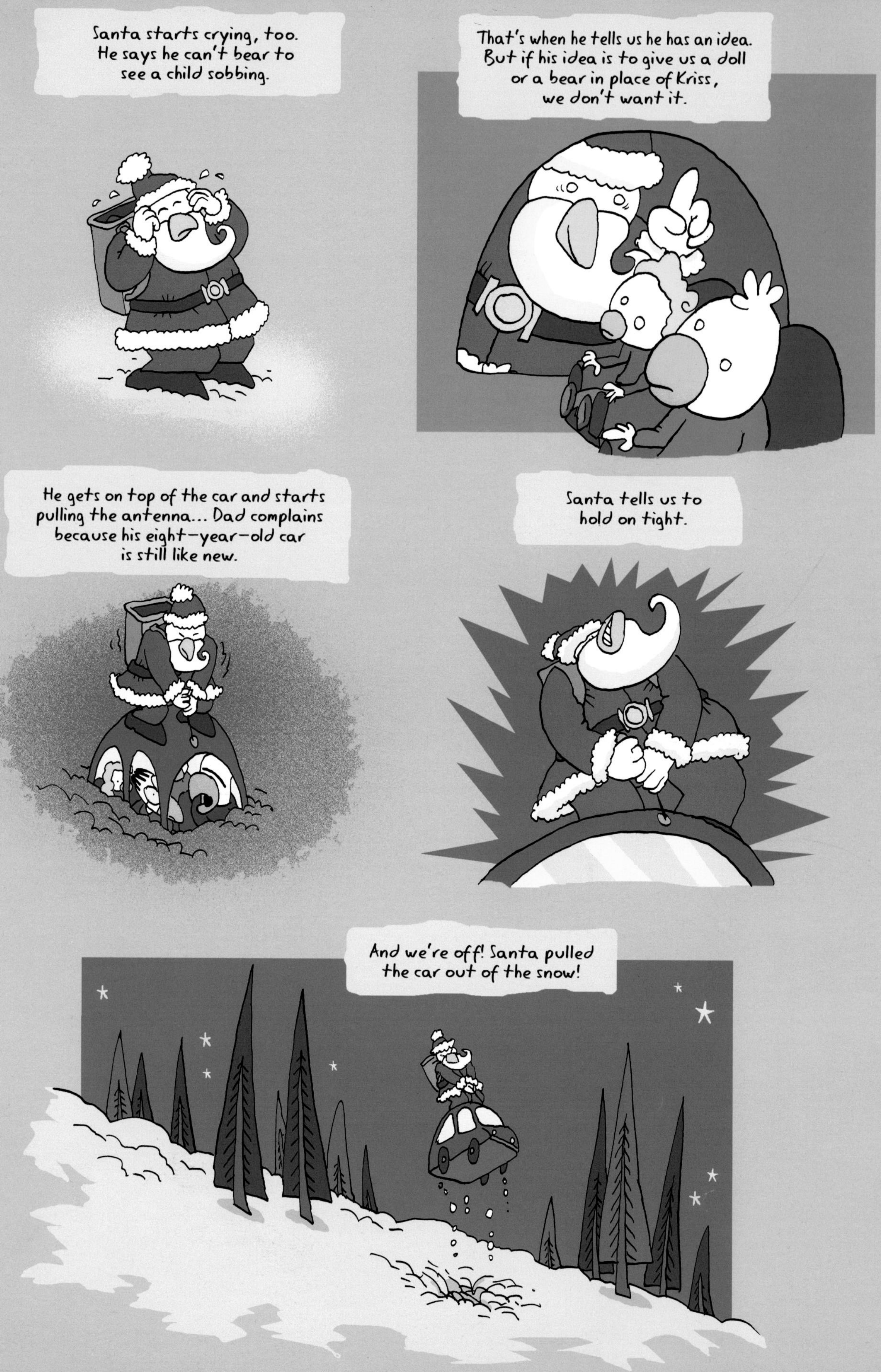
Santa starts crying, too. He says he can't bear to see a child sobbing.
That's when he tells us he has an idea. But if his idea is to give us a doll or a bear in place of Kriss, we don't want it.
He gets on top of the car and starts pulling the antenna... Dad complains because his eight-year-old car is still like new.
Santa tells us to hold on tight.
And we're off! Santa pulled the car out of the snow!

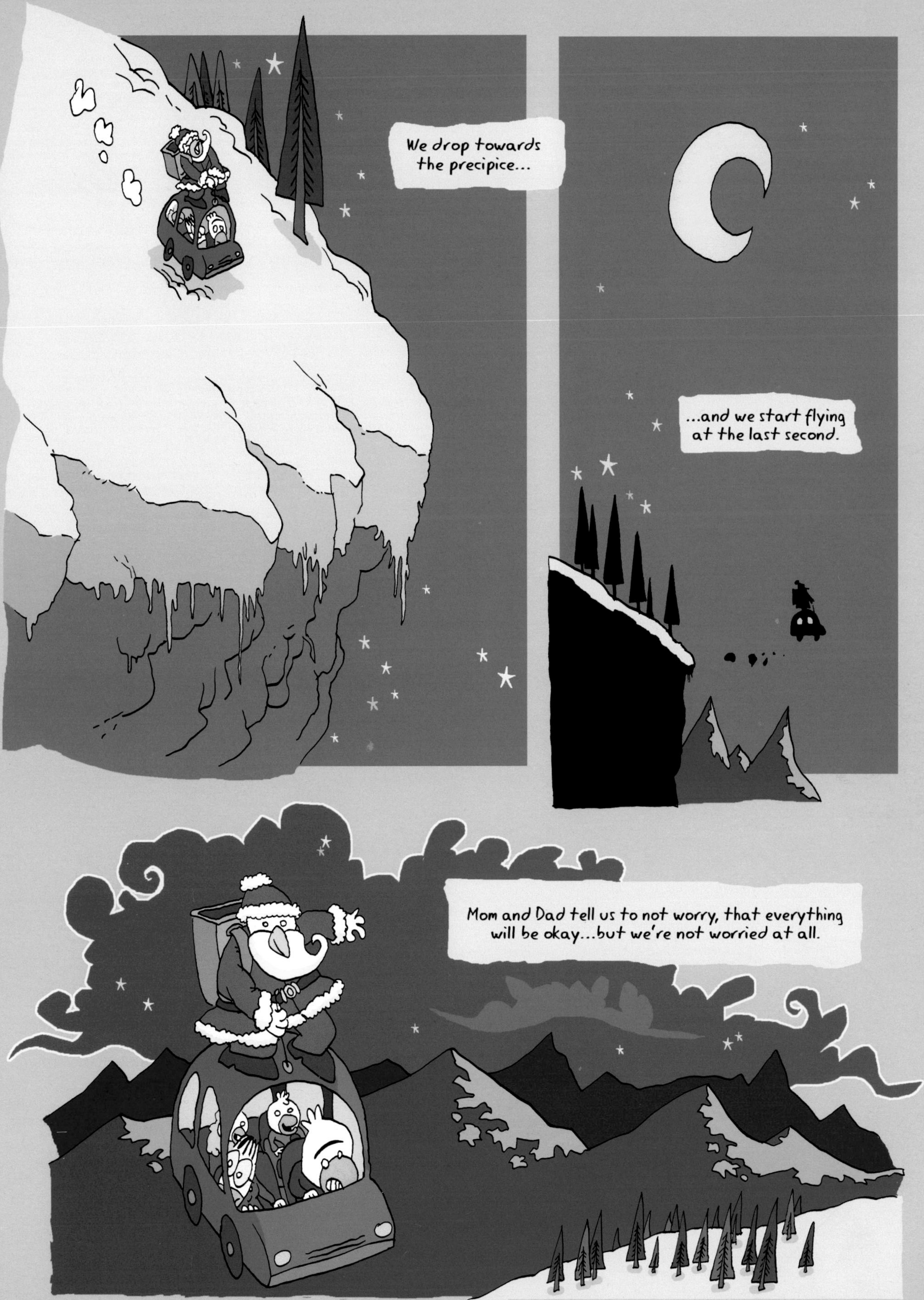
We drop towards the precipice...
...and we start flying at the last second.
Mom and Dad tell us to not worry, that everything will be okay...but we're not worried at all.

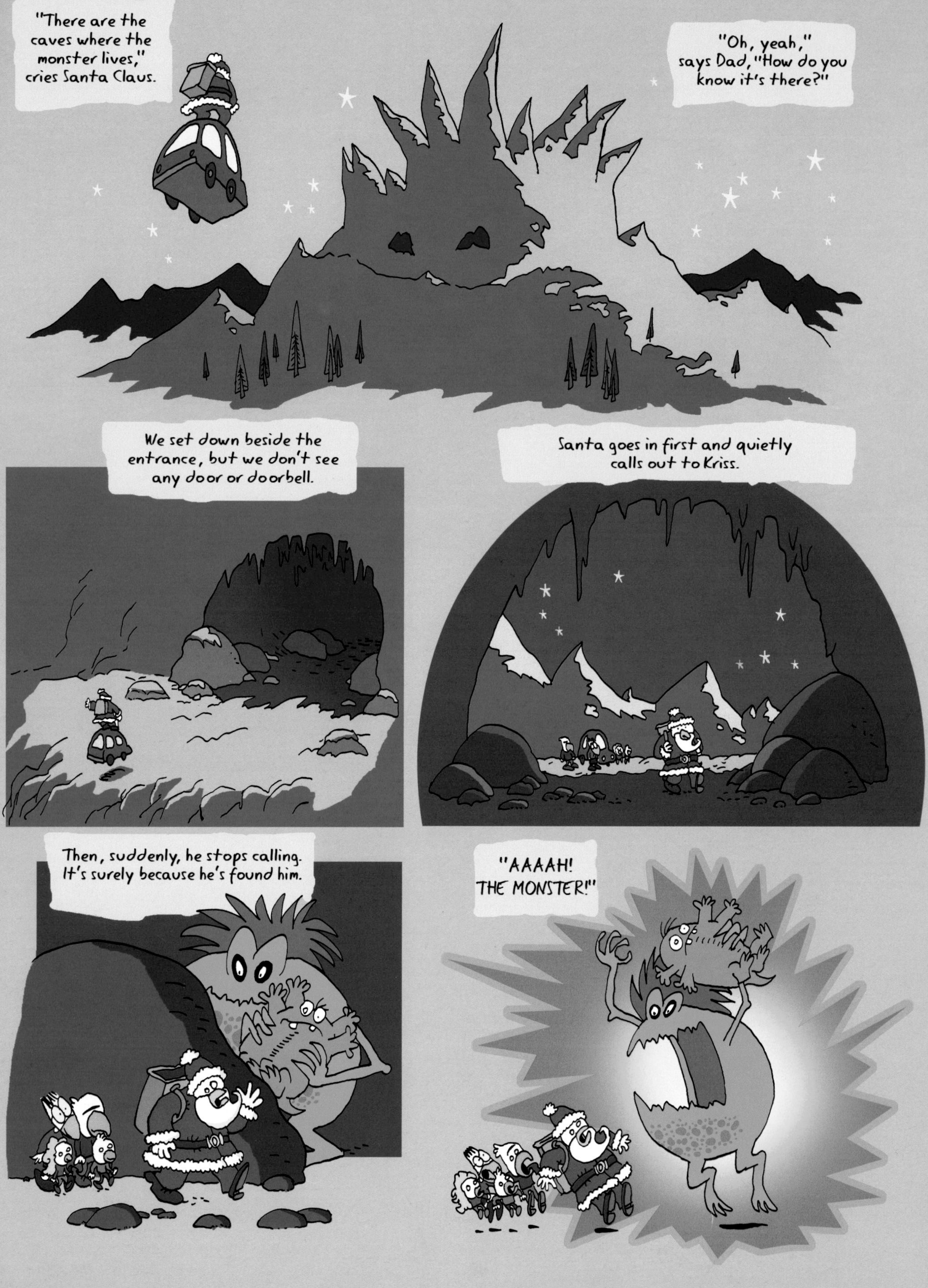

"There are the caves where the monster lives," cries Santa Claus.
"Oh, yeah," says Dad, "How do you know it's there?"
We set down beside the entrance, but we don't see any door or doorbell.
Santa goes in first and quietly calls out to Kriss.
Then, suddenly, he stops calling. It's surely because he's found him.
"AAAAH! THE MONSTER!"

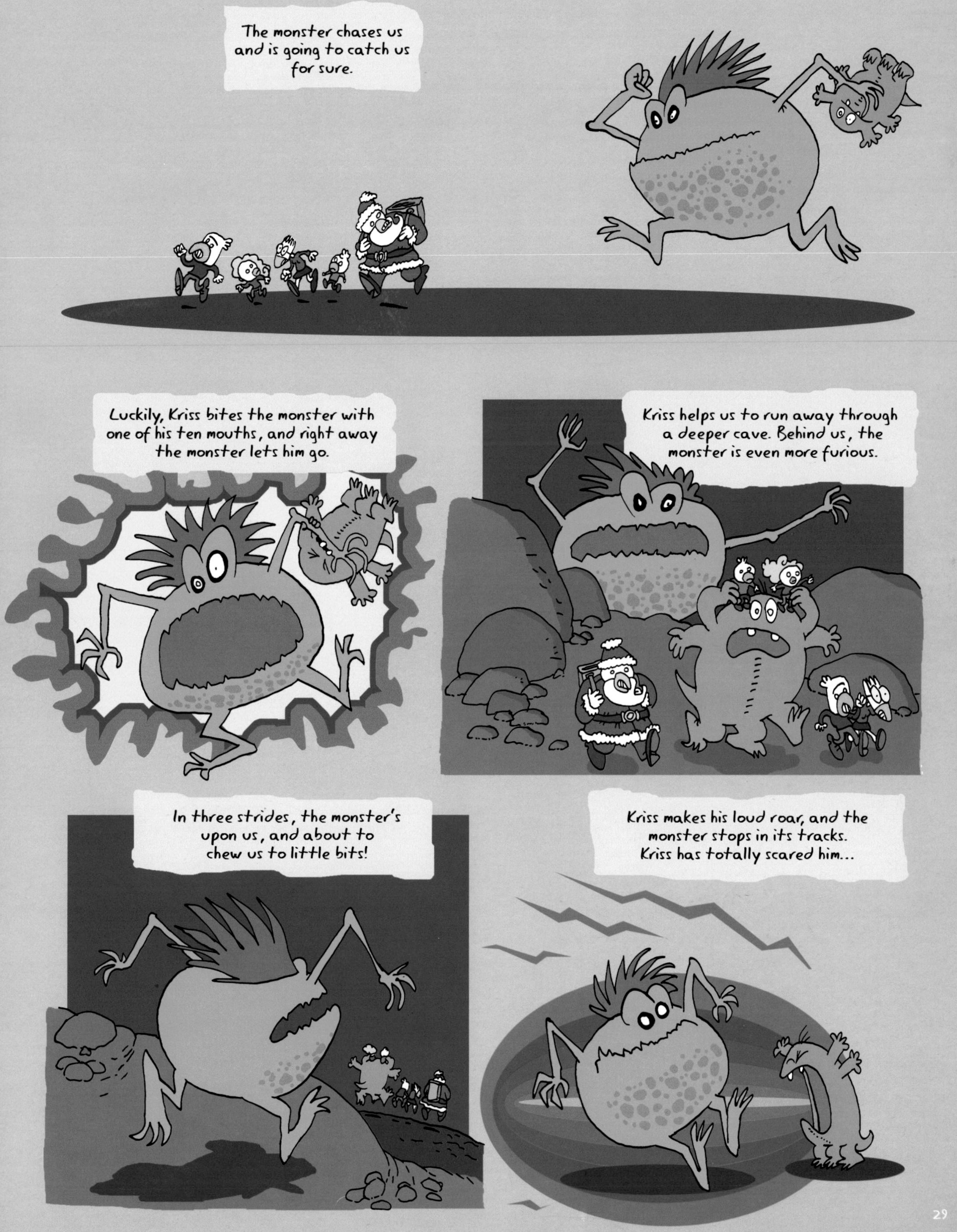
The monster chases us and is going to catch us for sure.
Luckily, Kriss bites the monster with one of his ten mouths, and right away the monster lets him go.
Kriss helps us to run away through a deeper cave. Behind us, the monster is even more furious.
In three strides, the monster's upon us, and about to chew us to little bits!
Kriss makes his loud roar, and the monster stops in its tracks. Kriss has totally scared him...

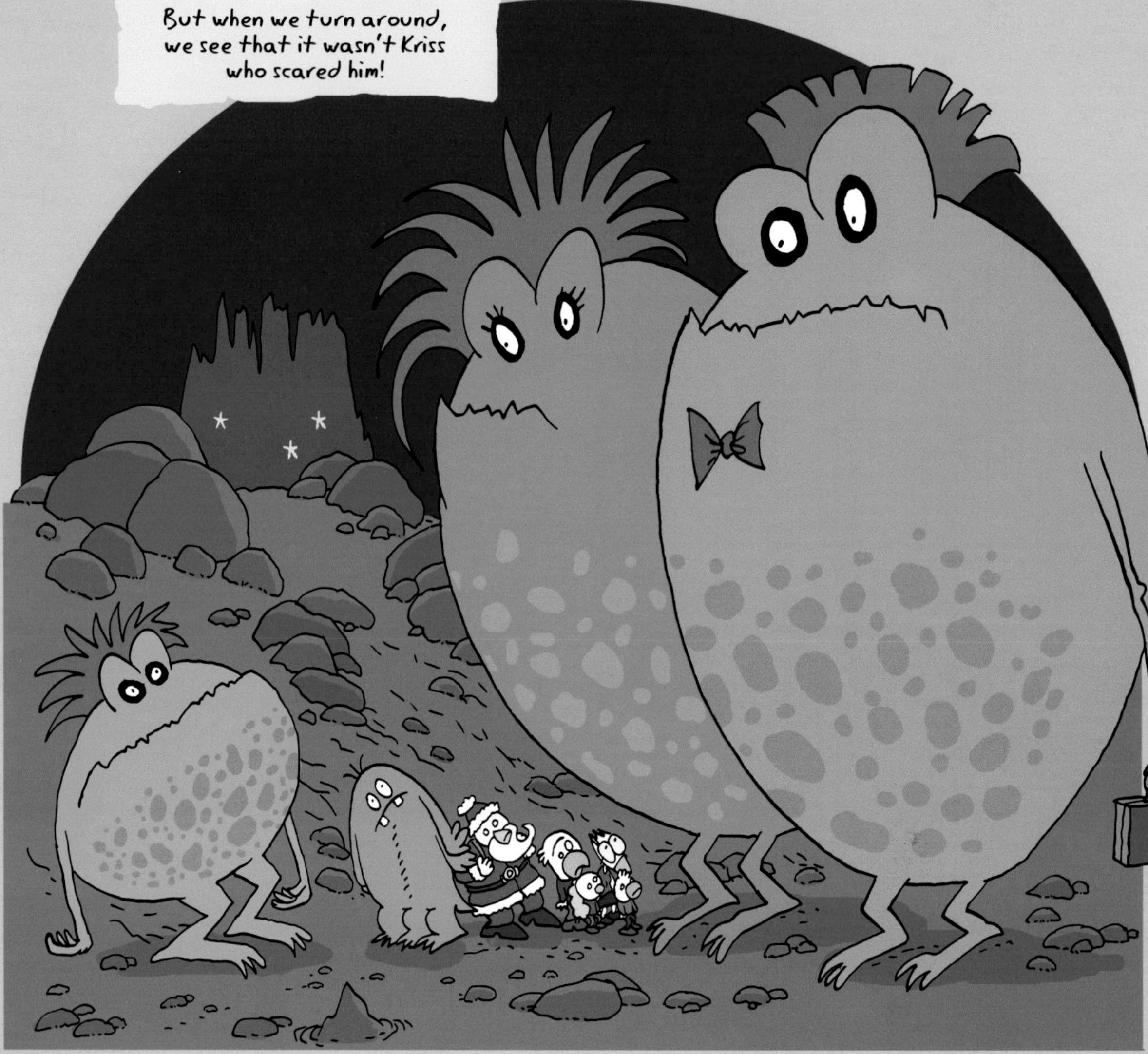
But when we turn around, we see that it wasn't Kriss who scared him!

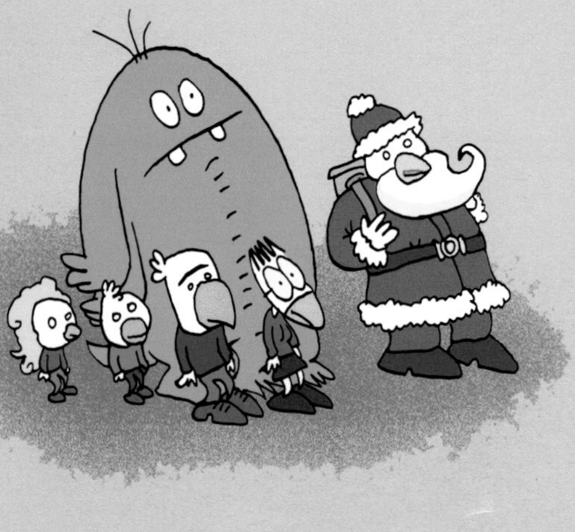
They're the monster's parents coming home from work. Santa Claus explains to them what has happened.

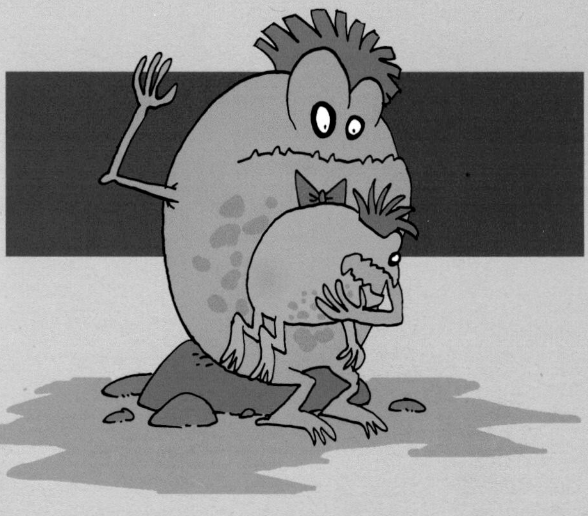
The monster's parents give their child a spanking, and we say he certainly deserved it.

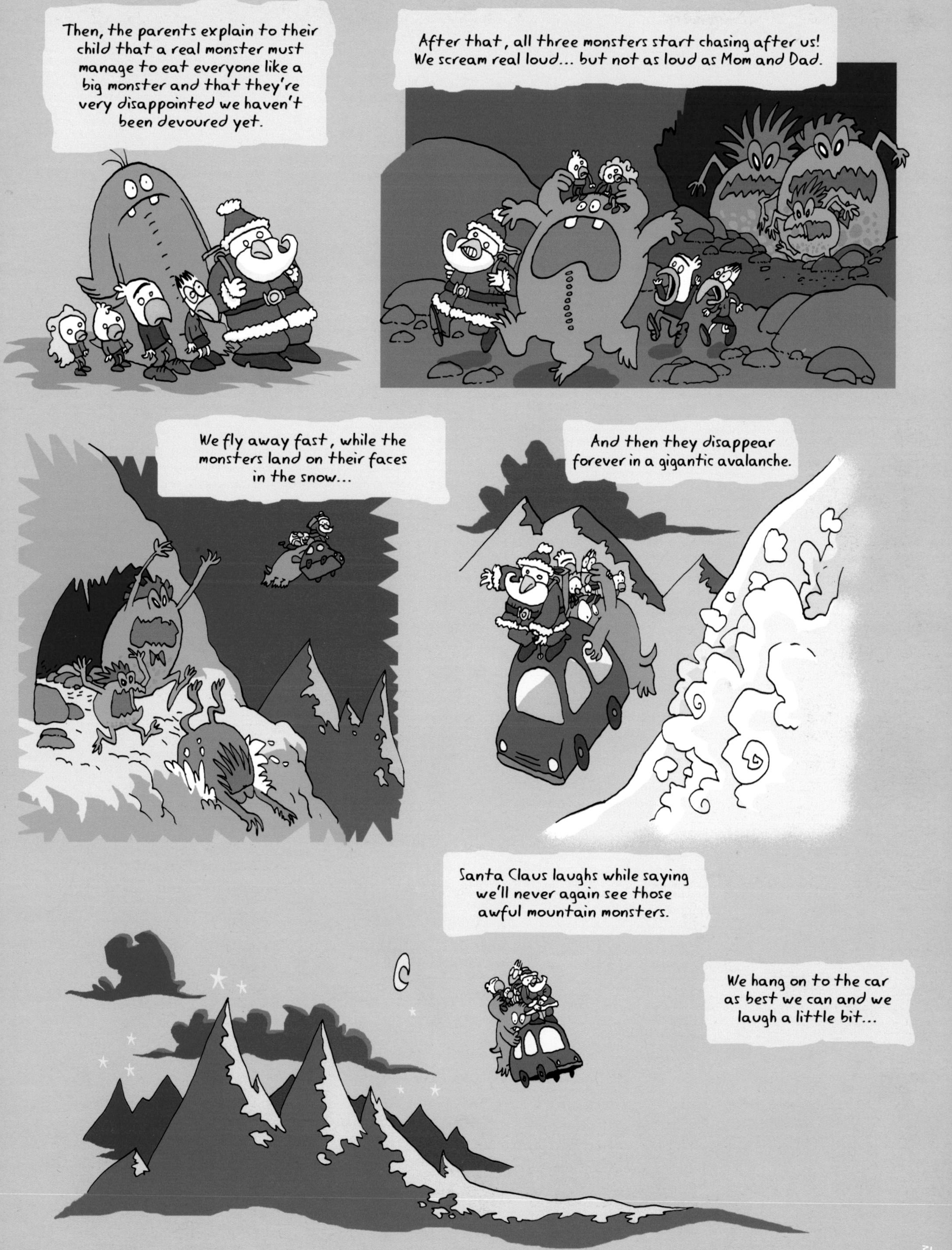

Then, the parents explain to their child that a real monster must manage to eat everyone like a big monster and that they're very disappointed we haven't been devoured yet.
After that, all three monsters start chasing after us! We scream real loud... but not as loud as Mom and Dad.
We fly away fast, while the monsters land on their faces in the snow...
And then they disappear forever in a gigantic avalanche.
Santa Claus laughs while saying we'll never again see those awful mountain monsters.
We hang on to the car as best we can and we laugh a little bit...

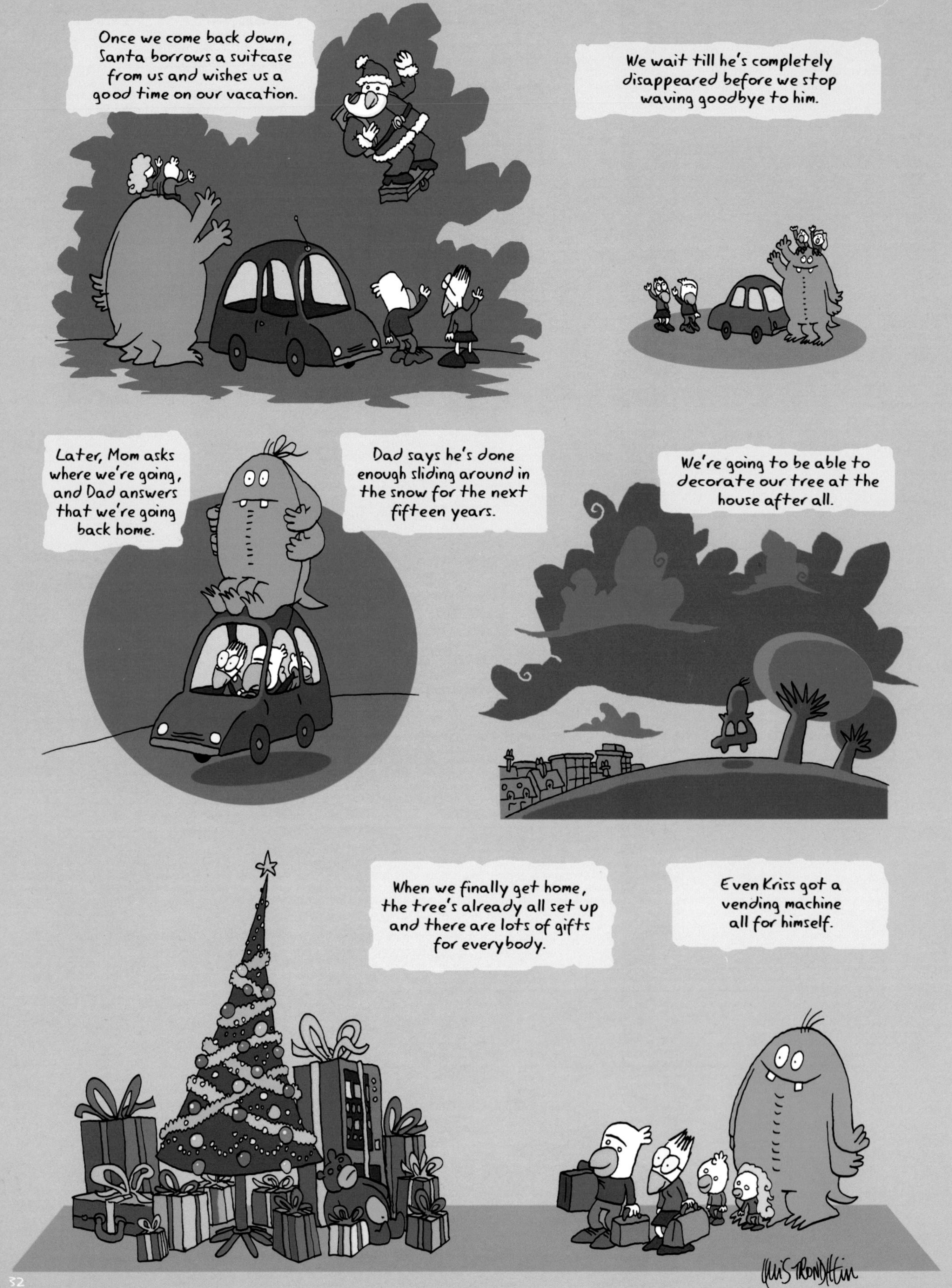
Once we come back down, Santa borrows a suitcase from us and wishes us a good time on our vacation.
We wait till he's completely disappeared before we stop waving goodbye to him.
Later, Mom asks where we're going, and Dad answers that we're going back home.
Dad says he's done enough sliding around in the snow for the next fifteen years.
We're going to be able to decorate our tree at the house after all.
When we finally get home, the tree's already all set up and there are lots of gifts for everybody.
Even Kriss got a vending machine all for himself.

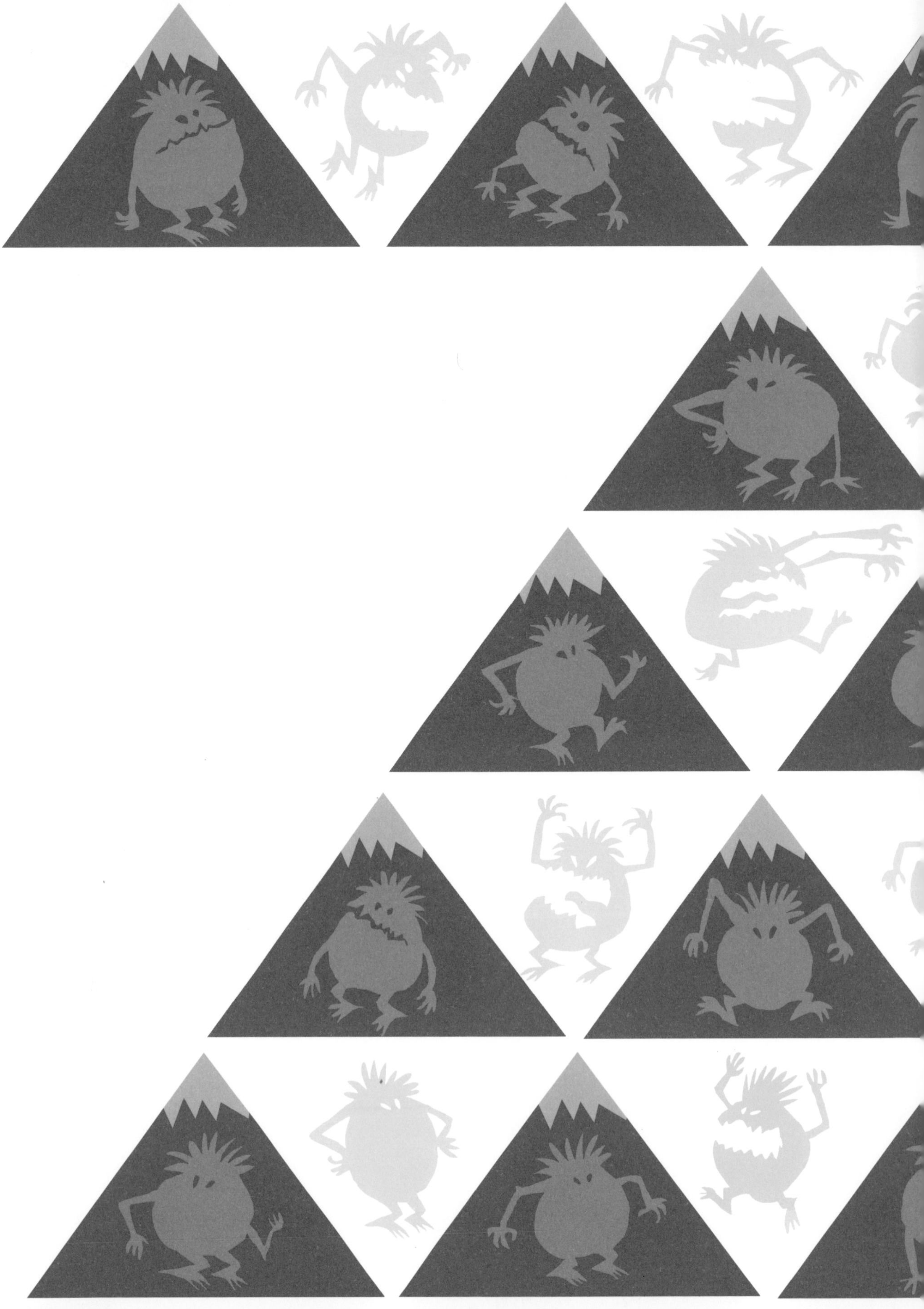